A tale of two Souls

Anand Kumar

INDIA • SINGAPORE • MALAYSIA

Notion Press

Old No. 38, New No. 6
McNichols Road, Chetpet
Chennai - 600 031

First Published by Notion Press 2019
Copyright © Anand Kumar 2019
All Rights Reserved.

ISBN: 978-1-64650-733-7

WHAT can I say about a twenty-three-year-old girl who had the dreams as vast as an ocean?

That she was beautiful. And ambitious. That she knew her heart better than anyone else and that inside her heart, there was a safe place for me. And that she loved playing badminton and listening to music as much as anything else. And that I left her, smiling, to let her tears disappear in front of me.

Here I am, two years later, sitting and wondering what I meant to her and where I stood in the list of things she loved.

"On the top of the list," she would have said, had I asked her two years ago.

I was there for her when she needed me, and I left her when she was longing for me. I gave her a lot of happy moments, to only let her drown in tears.

Memories accompanying me, I was travelling from Chennai to Bangalore in a train; back to the place I last saw her.

The last two years of my college was all about a journey that I scripted together with her. A journey that deserved to last a lifetime. I could have never imagined a day without her being around. Today, she was only a reminiscence. Albeit today, with the world keeping me busy, silence and loneliness befriended me. If ever there was a person whom I loved all my life, it was her. And I meant the world to her. My dormant life was thriving to swim in the midst of unabated memories. It took a while for me to understand my flaws, but I am glad I did. Little did I know that I would be going back to the place where it all ended?

As the fond memories and haunting thoughts, flipped like a toss of a coin, I felt like a lost soul amidst an ocean of crowd. It was July, and the rains during this time were common. A flower cast spell of rain droplets were on which painted an artistic view. It was only complemented by the train as it was entering into a tunnel. Her memories were brewing inside me and flashes of her was fluttering inside my heart. The ever-enthusiastic tea boys in the train were not able to shake me off from my mood. I was slipping into a parallel world of memories, only to be woken up to reality by the buzzing sounds of the conversations happening around me. Standing by the doors of the coaches in the train is one of my favourite pass times, and I stood right beside it, secluding myself from the rest of the crowd. The fresh air and fragrance of rural India greeted me into nostalgia, a world that was only present in my memories.

I was soon lost in deep thoughts as I slowly moved my hands over a foggy window and drew an 'X' over it. I cleared the fog over the window and looked at the trees flashing by. A soft and soothing melodious track was playing in my ears, with every word of the lyrics touching my heart. I wished I did not let it go this far. The feeling of losing her was wrenching my heart and with it; the burden of my own weight was increasing. A little drop of tear stayed stiff at the corner of my eyes. With my heart burning in desire, I stood there wondering if I could have changed those last few days between us.

Chapter One

I ALWAYS believed that simple moments could change our lives. Little did I know that it would be on this day, my life would never be the same again? Each hour and each moment of this day is vivid and fresh in my mind.

It was a rainy day, and I was at my college library when I first saw Sakshi. The weather, in all its bipolar glory, did not seem to make up its mind. The sun was playing a little game of hide and seek admits the clouds. The rains were on and off, and I found shelter inside the verandah of the college library. This was the first time I was at my college library. I hardly knew anyone over there. The rain was intense, and I was getting restless standing at one place for a long time. Even to move was getting difficult. The library itself was intimidating to look at. It was luring me to get in and have a look at it, and I acknowledged. The setup of the library was formal, colourful and stylish. The finely carved capitals were complemented by a great number of noteworthy antiques, and amongst them was a satinwood worktable. The books were well arranged on the antique wooden racks. The warmth of knowledge was felt all around the place. As I stood there, in the midst of an ocean of books, the place looked gracious.

The place was quiet, and no one out there was a face known to me. The sheer silence of the place, with an unknown crowd, shook the inertia for books in me. I ambled over each of the racks to figure out if I could find something interesting. The rains were unrelenting, parading a range of big sized drops. The sound of the rains falling on the windows was shattering. I had to grab a book to kill some time until the rain subsided. The sheer amount of books made it difficult to search. It was even harder when I had no clue what I wanted to read. It took a while, and after ambling through a few racks, I came across the book, *Love in the Southern Rains.*

The cover of the book was enticing enough to get me hooked. The library had a dedicated space for quick readers who could sit and read. I grabbed the book from the rack and walked down to the satinwood worktable. Around the table was a large wooden bench for people to sit. It was comfortable enough to spend a few hours reading.

The book was quite handy and had about one hundred and forty pages. It was unassuming. As the clock hands flicked its way through the numbers, and every little sound heard, I began to read the book. I was a few pages into it when I heard someone speaking to me.

"Excuse me," shot out a voice from behind me.

This was the first time I saw Sakshi. Her hair was arranged like a pack of threads, weaved in a straight line, thick, brown and long, neatly secured in place by a hairband and a few clips. The colour of her hair nicely complemented her fair skin and dark eyes. She had an oval face and was wearing a white top and blue jeans. She wasn't as tall, and not too short either, maybe around 5 feet 5 inches, and was wearing a blue colour sports shoe. Her attire was just about perfectly fitting her.

"Would you mind letting me know when you would finish reading the book?" she asked, pointing her fingers towards the book.

I stared at the book once again, and I had barely read the first few pages. The book was quite enticing, and I did not want to give it off without reading. But beyond that, thinking about it now, I could have as well given the book as well. Reading was not as much fun to me.

In a superior tone, I replied, "Well, it would take a couple of hours," and I put my head back to focusing on the book.

Destiny as it sounds, a little harsh to be blamed for, may have been different, if I never faked to be reading that goddamn book.

In a matter of seconds, her face turned pale. Her tone changed, and she moved a step towards me. "Listen. I need that goddamn book. I have been looking for it for a long time now," she said with her eyes firmly piercing through my eyes.

Her reaction to it was surprising, as I felt she could have waited for me to complete reading the book. Moreover, I had already started reading the book and it was only appropriate for her to wait.

"Well, you may have it, but not before I have had my hands on every single page of the book," I shot back with a smile.

She was staring at me. She seemed the arrogant and pushy type. Okay, maybe she wanted the book, but she would only have to wait, at least until when my superego subsidized.

"You have hardly started reading it. Haven't you?"

"I may have, but I did before you did."

I was in no mood to give up on this. I also had a lot of time which I needed to spend until the rain relented.

"You may have, but I have been wanting it, and I cannot wait for a couple of hours here," she protested.

My ego was being tested, and I did not want to give up all the more. I was never this type, but this conversation with a stranger was an exploration of myself.

I am not sure if it was pity, or it was her, I felt that she had some genuine reason for wanting the book.

What if she had some important work later on? I thought.

I looked at her and said, "Listen, I don't mind, coming to you, wherever you are, and giving you the book. But all this only after I have read the book completely."

In the pause that ensued, I was glad that I gave myself an opportunity to meet her again.

She sighed in disbelief and shook her head twice.

"What the hell makes you think, I would agree to this?" she asked.

I smiled, leaned towards the desk, looked straight into her eyes, and said, in a tone that would best be described as sarcasm.

"Because you are the one needing the book, and this is the only chance of you getting this today."

Her looks were intimidating, and I was not the one to be reacting to it. She backed out, turned around and walked a couple of steps. As she was about to get out of my sight, she paused, had a quick look at her watch, and then saw me.

"And, how can I be sure you would come and give it to me?" she asked.

The vibe in my mind got to me at that instance. I wanted to win this conversation. The rush of the moment drove me to do something silly.

I instantly took the key of my bike from my pocket in a single go, placed it on the desk and said, "You can have my bike if I don't come to you and give you the book."

The part about being a winner is the risk you take in becoming a good loser. It was only after placing the key on the desk, that I realized what I had done. I was now hoping that she wouldn't accept the deal. I couldn't retract my words or my action. When I looked at the book, my spine was feeling horrible at the thought of having owed my bike for a book.

The one thing I was hoping would not happen, happened, as she turned back and walked straight towards me. The expression on her face changed, and a cunning little smile emerged. She saw me, eye to eye, lunged forward and said, "Tough luck, pal. I may not need the book anymore," and to my agony, she took the key and walked away.

And I sat there, looking at her as she walked into the rain. Out of nowhere, I burdened myself. As she was about to get out of my sight, she turned back, with the keys hanging in her hand, she looked at me and said, "Two hours, and if I don't get the book, this would be mine."

I ran my fingers through my hairs and let out a frustrated sigh, looking around at all the people in the library. I was looking like a fool and was feeling embarrassed. I covered my face with my hands in shame and cursed myself.

I must confess that I was blown away by her attitude. I did not know her name, neither had I seen her in all those two years at the college. How would I even find her? What if she left the college in the two hours and went home or somewhere? What if I didn't find her? All that I had in my mind at the moment was her image. But then, how would I even describe her to my friends if I needed their help? They would laugh at my foolishness. Lots of what-ifs were creeping in my mind, and it cast an iota of doubt within me. I liked the challenge though and quietly wondered if I had scored a few marks in her mind.

ক্ষ্

Two hours on and by now the rains had a little mercy and settled into a breeze of tiny droplets pleasing every loving soul. I could have begun searching for her immediately, but then, it would only mean that I had not read the book. I didn't want to look silly yet again.

Opposite to the library and a few steps away was our college canteen. This was one place where you would give yourself the highest probability to find someone. I was thirsty as well, and I wanted to drink something. I bought my favourite mango juice and drank it in a single go. I gave me some energy. The cool weather helped me to relax. I went to the washroom and splashed water on to my face. The rain, drizzle, and cold meant that I needed to get something hot to eat. I went to the counter again to get some chat. As I picked it up and walked towards the dining table, I heard somebody calling out my name.

"Maybe you will come out of your thoughts sometime today, Rahul."

His voice might have sounded stern to an outsider, but Kabir and I had become good friends. I am not sure when, but at some point, while I was a regular visitor to the canteen, our casual interactions blossomed into a warm friendship. He respected my opinions, and I treasured his. He had a lot of stories to talk about. Kabir was someone who had a strong Hindi accent in his English. He was a little bit lumpy to look at with his round face and short stature. From whatever I could figure out of him, he was cold at heart. He would give you suggestions that only he could think of, off the blue.

"What is the matter, bro?" he asked politely.

I was torn away from my thoughts, and I took a deep breath. His soft black eyes were holding mine, with a politeness to it. I stayed quite, as I was gathering a lot of thoughts and was trying to put them together.

"Rahul…"

"Yes, baba. I am listening," I said.

"No, you are not," he said, pouting.

I didn't react. He walked up to me and placed his elbows on my shoulders.

I looked at him and into his eyes, trying to see myself. I felt a little ashamed to say it to him. But I needed someone's help. I was not sure if I could find her all by myself.

"There is this girl. I saw her in the library today."

I closed my eyes for a second.

"Hmm…" he nodded as he crushed a big bite of a samosa between his teeth.

"I need to find her, and I was wondering how I could."

My words sounded hesitant to his ears, but understandably so. He didn't react a lot.

"What's her name?" he asked.

"I don't know," I said, frowning.

He smiled, which seemed more of a giggle. He placed his mobile phone on the table.

"So, you don't know the name of the person you are searching for. And I would also assume you don't know any details about her," he remarked.

I wished he was not right this time around, but alas, he was spot on.

"Hmmm," I replied. By now, I was feeling a little uncomfortable with this conversation.

There weren't many people around, and my eyes were rolling to every corner, hoping to find her somewhere. With each passing minute, the headcount was increasing, but I couldn't find her.

Kabir was observing my behaviour without saying a word. My eyes and mind were not at one place. They kept looking for her. And finally, after a few seconds, it met the smiling Kabir. I exactly knew what he was thinking about me right now. I was behaving like a small kid who was in search of my favourite chocolate.

"Kabir bro. Listen. I do not know anything about her. All that I know her is by her face, and I need to find her," I replied in an emphatic tone, turned around and was about to leave the place.

"Rahul, can you describe her looks. I can try and figure out if I can find out with the people I know."

I closed my eyes and saw her through my memory. I found her eyes. How would I describe her eyes? Except that they were soft and black. And had bundles of expressions within them.

One thing that I knew, for sure, they had truth in them. And that is what I trusted.

৵৽

It had been an hour now since I started searching, and by now, I was losing confidence in finding her.

"For sure, I am a loser now," I murmured. I had been to every corner of the campus and yet I was unable to find her.

Was she playing with me?

What if she had forgotten about the book and left the campus?

Lots of questions were beating through my brain.

There was a little hope left within me, and I felt very tired. It was then, at a distance, I saw the Embassy Sports complex. Our college sports campus was very huge and was located at the far end of campus. It hosts a lot of sports facilities. The place is always lively, as there would be one or the other sports competitions going on out there. Today it was the turn for badminton. The setup of the complex itself would suggest nothing. It was an age-old building, pale and discoloured paints all over the place.

Although I loved playing sports, I had hardly been playing at the campus though. I was there only when I took a walkthrough of the campus during my admission. I felt crazy about the day. It was taking me to places I had hardly been in the last two years. It was as if, I was playing a game of treasure chest, and that the treasure was something more than a game.

There wasn't anything that suggested her presence out there. It was my heart and the little hope within it that convinced me to enter the complex. Unable and unwilling to walk or even stand, I dragged my half-worn out body to the sports complex like a snail.

It took a while for me to read the canvas poster at the entrance of the complex. It was about the intercollege badminton tournament that was going on.

Was she the sports type?

Would she be there watching the matches?

What are my chances of finding her inside?

Lots of questions, yet again as I egged myself to enter the campus.

The first look about the density of people at that place was disappointing. For a college of about eight hundred-odd students, there were only about thirty or forty who had come to watch the game. Our college was never good with sports. Despite having great facilities, there was a lack of encouragement. At best, we would end up being the runners up in a tournament.

Students chose the Oscar Institute of Technology, OIT, for the quality of education and its facilities. The placement opportunities was another reason OIT was popular. It was not a big shock for me to see the number of people who had turned up for the match.

With the number of people being so low, whatever little hope I had, turned into hopelessness. I gave in with despair, and already was wondering how I would go back home today.

I was searching for reasons to tell my parents when they figure out about my missing bike.

"My ego hurt me today," I said to myself.

I was going mad at myself and could not stop cursing myself. I turned towards the crowd, with one last attempt to find her. Scanning thirty-odd faces does not take much time, and in a few seconds, as expected, I could not find her. I let out an exaggerated sigh of pain, "God, I messed it up. This is torture."

"Rahul, we are up to something special. Don't you think so?" someone whispered to me.

I turned around to find Maahi. She walked from a few seats behind and came closer to me.

Maahi was one of my close friends. She is a trusted, ever happy person with a wide smile. Five of us were always together, be it in classes or otherwise, and Maahi was one amongst them. It was always easy to be comfortable with her. When someone is feeling low, Maahi would be the one who would provide comforting support.

"Three more points, and we will have a badminton champion for the first time from our college," she said while keeping her eyes glued on the game. I was not in the mood to give the game a thought, but then the sportsperson in me gave in a kick.

"Nothing to lose," I said to myself.

During my schooling days, I had represented my state at the national table tennis championship meet.

The LED scoreboard placed at the corner of the court read:

1 set all, Sakshi (OIT) 18 – Jyotsna (BIT) 16.

Students from about twenty-five colleges take part in this tournament. And I found it astonishing to see that someone from our college was playing a final. It was all the more surprising to see her in a position to win the championship. She was leading in the final set and three points away from the championship. This had never happened before, and might never happen again.

My focus now shifted towards the game as I looked at the court. The bike, the book, and the girl was out of my mind for the moment. I started cheering along with the crowd in support for Sakshi.

Chapter Two

NOT even in my freakiest of imaginations, did it ever occur that the one I had been searching for was the one representing our college at the finals. I wondered if reading a novel had anything to do with playing a final. I could only smile at myself and let out a big sigh of relief.

A bad guess but a lucky scalp.

I found her, after all.

I joined the bandwagon of cheers with more conviction now and took part in the chanting chorus.

Sakshi was stretching her opponent, playing the shuttle to all the corners. She seemed in total control of the game up until then before she went for an ambitious cross-court smash. It looked very close to the line. The umpire called it 'out', and she protested in vain. The score now read '18–17'.

"She is last year's champion," Maahi screamed into my ears to make sure I heard her.

Jyotsna, Sakshi's opponent, was a tall and a fit girl. From the way she moved around the court, it was obvious that she was a professional. She was quick on her feet and had a well-formulated technique that could dismiss any opponent.

"Okay. She plays like a pro," I replied with affirmation.

"Yes, she plays in club leagues and won a lot of tournaments," Maahi replied.

The tension was brewing on everyone's face. A lot of cheering and clapping was on. Thirty-odd people, but the noise felt a lot beyond. Jyotsna seemed a little cool. She was the experienced one and knew what it took to be a champion. The sweat and tension was visible on Sakshi's face, and she was ready to break. She was nervous.

Out of nowhere, Maahi turned towards me, tapped my shoulders, and said, "What made our hero come here?"

I was sincerely hoping to avoid that question. But despite the tension, Maahi did not forget to ask me that question. To keep the unnecessary focus away, I replied in a casual tone with a sheepish smile, "The sportsman in me."

I did not understand the look she gave me in that moment. One thing was for sure, she did not believe my answer.

"The match is getting closer, right?" I said, trying to wade off any attention.

She nodded her head and said, "Yes, looks like today is a day for the unexpected to happen."

Street smart is what everyone would regard her as. She would always understand things without crossing her limits. She judged that I would not give her an answer, but at the same time, she guessed that I came in there for someone. All that Maahi was not sure off was for whom I was there.

In the meantime, the game continued, and two unforced errors followed from Sakshi. The score read '18–19'.

She was exhausted and tired. The previous rally lasted for about twenty shots apiece. Jyotsna seemed fitter of the two, and she had a massive advantage with her height as well. The reach was better with Jyotsna, and she needed a fewer amount of steps to get to the shuttle.

Sakshi opted to take a drink break. It was the right thing to do, especially when you have lost your radar and need to get back your focus. She took a deep breath or two. Being a sportsperson myself, it was easier to sense what was going on in her mind. I had been through such situations during my table tennis days, and they were not easy. Then again, these are the reasons why you would love to play a sport.

"She is a newcomer to the college. The burden is far too high on her shoulders," Maahi said.

"Okay. No wonder, I haven't seen her all these days," I replied.

"She is nervous and trying too hard. She wants to win this."

I could not avoid feeling for her. She was far from being relaxed and was not willing to look at the crowd. She gulped in some water and wiped the sweat on her forehead. She took some time to tighten her hairs and then jogged back to the court. She closed her eyes once before she took the position to receive the serve.

"Maybe the biggest game for her thus far," Maahi said as she still kept her cheerful claps going on.

I nodded and replied, "Maybe."

By now, the word about the match spread across the college. The thirty-odd crowd had doubled quickly, and the cheers got louder. Everyone wanted Sakshi to win.

As the game restarted, her feet started to move well again, and she seemed to be in top gear. This time, she was the aggressor of the two, and she pushed her opponent. First, to the back right court, stretching her, and she followed it up with a deft drop onto the left. The crowd found its voice back, and the score read, '19–19'.

It was now Sakshi's turn to serve, and she chose to go to her favourite backhand serve. Was it the tension that moved her, or was it the sweat in her palm? She rode no luck, and the shuttle landed into the net. She lost her serve, and with that, the scoreboard read, '19–20'. There was disbelief on everyone's face followed by a sound of oooooos. The rare chance for OIT was now slipping away.

Everyone stood still. Silence was all over, and the tension was gripping. A lot more of sweat was dripping from Sakshi's forehead as Jyotsna was keeping her opponent wait longer. That is what you call experience in sport. When you know your opponent is struggling, keep them waiting longer, so that they make the mistakes.

After a few seconds, Jyotsna was ready to serve and chose to go for a long serve to the backcourt. A safe option under these situations. Both of them started the rally playing safe and curbed themselves from taking risks. One shot was followed by another, and after about eight long tosses, Jyotsna sent one crashing into the body of Sakshi. With that, Jyotsna lept with joy, and the hearts of everyone was broken. Besides, with the defeat, the hopes of OIT went crashing as well.

There was a stunned silence in the court until one sportive heart chose to applaud the players. One followed another, and soon, everyone was clapping. Everyone at the ground was enduring the beauty of sport. Sakshi was broken, even more at heart. She had no energy left inside her. She gave her best.

She dragged herself back and walked up to Jyotsna to shake hands with and congratulate her. The two players hugged each other before they walked away. Both were destined to be winners. Jyotsna may have won the game, but it was Sakshi, who stole hearts.

Her attitude was admirable, and I stood there admiring the way she was carrying herself out of the defeat. She very well knew how disappointed everyone was. She thanked everyone who came to support her, and she did look a little pale and out of complexion.

It took a while for her to breathe freely. Her friends, a very few of them, were there trying to comfort her. She needed space, and she was not getting it. She stood there talking to everyone who walked up to her to either console or congratulate. Winning does not come easy, but what comes harder is the power to withstand the pain of losing. She was exhibiting the power that was firmly within her.

I stood there, waiting for everyone to leave the place.

"Rahul, are you coming?" Maahi asked.

"You carry on," I murmured.

Maahi gave me a stare as she walked out.

"I will join you people in a while," I turned towards Maahi and said to her.

She kept quiet and continued to walk.

In a few minutes, almost everyone left the place. Sakshi was packing her badminton racquets and placing them into her kit bag. Her friends left one after another as she took a couple of minutes for herself. I waited patiently.

She drank some more water and was now heading towards the exit. She put up a very brave face, despite her defeat. She deserved to be proud. Her strides, as she started to walk off, got better as if to say, "I will get her next time."

As she started walking towards the direction of the exit, I too walked in the same direction. But, with some hesitation. I was not sure if she noticed me, both during the match or after. It was at the exit that we faced up with each other.

⁊∘⁊

Rains, and how much I love them. It started to pour once again, hard enough to make the pitter-patter noise and keep us confined inside the complex. I offered my hands to shake, and she accepted it with some grace. For the moment, it was not about the keys or the book. All I wanted was to appreciate her for the way she fought. I wondered if I had the courage in me to accept a hard-fought defeat in an admirable way. She did it, and I felt it. Wow.

What would make her feel better now? I wondered. I made a few imaginative words to speak if I managed to find her. But now, the words were hard to come out of me. Silence emerged between us and I knew that she waited to hear from me. I muscled some voice out of my mouth to throw out a few at her, "That was indeed a great game."

She smiled and said, "Thank you."

A small dimple on her cheeks lit her smile, and even they looked gracious.

She continued, "So, you found me."

Well, I wanted to tell her, "For the rest of my life."

I looked away from her and drew my attention to the rains. The quietness reappeared as if to say we had nothing more to converse. I was unsure of how to react to her statement, and I felt being quiet was the best way to go about it. There was something magical in her words and her voice, and I was feeling nervy.

After a few quiet minutes, I opened the zip of my bag, took the book out, and offered it to her. The calm face of hers drew a small smile once again, and she gave the bike key back to me.

Oh my god. This is like, really insane, is exactly how I felt.

It would be appropriate if I said that. I froze every single time the dimple on her cheeks emerged. I wished to see them more often and was quietly praying for the rains, to continue. I wanted to be with her longer. The moment itself was overwhelming for me. My instincts got to me as I said, "Would you mind if I ask you to come for a coffee?"

With a pleasing stare, and the look of her eyes drawing me towards her, like a magnet, she said, "What if I said no?"

I looked at the rains again, and then drew my attention back to her, this time with an assured smile and replied, "I knew you would not say no."

She raised her eyebrows and with that her dimple vanished, she replied, "Overconfidence."

"Nah. A gut feel."

"What makes you think I would agree?"

I wanted to say, 'destiny', but I preferred to look at the rains.

Chapter Three

SHIPBAY, a milk bar close to our college, has been one of my favourite hangouts. The interiors of the restaurant were cozy, with a lot of bean bags coupled with sofas. The low hanging lights were always a treat. They were spaced equidistant from one another and arranged in a single line. The interiors of the restaurant had lots of ancient wooden antique items. The feel of the restaurant was enhanced with the fragrance of sandalwood agarbathis. Although the restaurant had a traditional feel, they had a lot of coffee varieties in their menu.

Sakshi and I sat across a small rounded wooden table, meant for two people. I offered for her to order the items from the menu card which was on the table.

It took a quick glance for her to say, "A filter coffee would do for me."

"You know what? The sandwiches are great out here, and would you like to try one." I offered her.

She took a couple of seconds to rethink and said, "Hmmm… okay."

A few minutes of silence endured, as both of us were looking up to another for a topic to converse on. The waiter then landed up in front of us to take the order. I placed the order for two filter coffee and two vegetarian sandwiches.

I looked at her, and she was fiddling with the tissues on the table.

"Rahul, second year, ECE," I said.

"Sakshi," she replied. "First year."

"Information and Technology," she added.

In the pause that ensued, I gave an inward thanks to her for joining me for the coffee.

"I am sorry for how I behaved in the morning," she said.

"I should have waited until you completed reading the book," she added.

She seemed honest with her apology and meant it. I shrugged the topic off.

"I was not put off anyway, so no worries," I replied in a polite manner.

"My super ego didn't let me give the book back then. My mistake," I added.

She smiled and nodded her head, and after that, things went pretty quiet, again.

Could we have run out of conversation so quickly? We sat there, smiling at each other every time our eyes met. Beyond that, we had nothing to talk about. I felt the urge to do something but was not able to figure out what. This was new to me.

By then, the waiter served the coffee and the sandwich. The coffee provided just the right warmth to my cold hands. It seemed as if both of us were more interested in the coffee rather than speaking to one another. The thought of her finding me a boring person was unsettling me and I had to take it on me to get the conversation going.

"So, are you a trained player?" I asked, hoping to start a conversation.

"I wouldn't call myself a trained player. When I was ten, I started off under a trainer for a couple of years," she answered.

"Now, I am on my own," she added.

"That's kind of cool," I said while munching a piece of the sandwich. After I swallowed the piece, I continued, "You were quite good at it. Like a pro."

She placed the coffee mug on the table, relaxed her body, and asked, "What about you?"

I smiled, and I replied, "To be honest, I was actually waiting for this question."

She laughed and said, "Okay, go on."

"I do some music, like playing the guitar and sometimes vocals."

"Occasionally though," I added.

Her eyebrows lit up. And she quizzed, "Hmm, like in concerts?"

"Not the big ones, but yes, the smaller ones," I said.

"That's nice. So, are you part of some band?" she asked.

"Not part of any band, but more like a freelancer."

"That is something new to me. A freelance guitarist," she said with a grin.

I am someone who is not good at masking my pride. I continued to unleash my accomplishments, hoping that she didn't take me lightly. I did not want to look small in front of her.

"In my schooling days, I was fond of playing table tennis. I played several tournaments. I also qualified to represent the south zone at the nationals," I said with some pride.

"That's nice. Do you still play?" she asked.

"Not really. It has been three years since I quit the game. I kept losing, studies followed, and I had to be out of the circuit," I replied and added, "Didn't enjoy it and gave it up."

Silence followed, yet again. She was shaking her head, which probably was a sign of disgust. No one who loves sport will accept lame reasons for quitting a game. She was no different.

After a few minutes, she poured some water from the jug on to a glass and sipped it. She stared at me for a while and asked, "What's left in you, for the game?"

The thought of someone quitting a game was probably hurting her. I put my head down in disgrace and replied, "Just an occasional player."

She was not impressed by it, and I was being a disappointment in this conversation. I knew it. For the first time, I felt bad about quitting the game. I felt all the more bad about talking about it as well. There was no need for this topic.

Silence endured once again, and outside the window, the rains continued to bash up. I wished our first conversation did not end on a negative note, but for sure, it was heading in that direction. A subject to another conversation needed deep thinking, and I was clueless.

I didn't want to talk about her match, but then, I needed a topic, and I had to talk about it.

"Today, you were hurt, weren't you?" I asked her.

She took her eyes off the rain and looked at me, and then looked away.

"No…" she said with a shiver in her voice. "Not really."

I didn't want to stress on it too much and decided to let the subject go away and said, "Good."

But then she interrupted me, and continued speaking, "I wanted to win it for the college."

By now, a tiny drop of a tear was lingering at the corner of her eye, and she was trying her best to hide it from me.

"So many people were cheering for me. I have not faced such a thing before. And I failed them," she uttered.

I looked into her eyes and said, "You may have not won the game, but you won a lot of hearts today," I assured her and continued, "That is worth a lot more."

She shut her eyes, and let her teardrop come out. She took her handkerchief and wiped it out and gave no more responses. I knew it was not the right topic to be conversing about. By then, the rains relented, and our coffee cups went dry, welcoming us to leave. The waiter produced the bill, and I paid it. We had to leave, and we shook hands.

"Thank you for the coffee," she said.

I tried to be formal once again, and I replied, "Thanks for joining me," and we both left.

As she was walking towards the bus stop, I called her out and asked, "Sakshi, when do we meet again?"

With a witty smile, she replied, "God willing."

Part of being a winner is the ability to be a good loser. There is no paradox involved. Maybe she did still have the upper hand between the two of us, but then, I liked playing the underdog.

Chapter Four

Destiny is a well-written script, directed by someone, who knows how to play the game of instincts. It was destined for us to bang into each other without having to wait for a long time.

This time, we got to meet at the college canteen. For our gang, the college canteen was a kind of hangout place. If the lecturer was absent, the first thing we did was to walk down to the college canteen. One or the other would have usually skipped breakfast, and this was the opportunity to make up for it. The moment someone buys a plate of whatever food, all would pounce on it at once.

Three days later, on a bright sunny day, the canteen was crowded than usual. There were no empty seats inside the canteen. We picked our food and beverages and walked outside the canteen.

Our canteen building is surrounded by big trees, and there are benches around each of them for people to sit. When the weather is cool, most of them preferred sitting outside at those benches. Likewise, when it is hot, people preferred to stay indoors. It was a herculean task of getting out of the canteen along with your cup of tea without littering a single drop.

For the kind of friends that we were, fun and laughter were always natural during our conversations. Whatever and whoever was the topic of conversation, it would not end without someone pulling in a joke.

The funniest in the group was Ajay, who was plump looking and a little short as well. Every time, he adjusted his spectacles, we knew he was up to something creepy. Priya, one of the tallest amongst the girls in our class, was the most assertive one. It was almost impossible to get her to change something she had already decided. Even if it was a small subject, she wouldn't give in to someone's ideas or opinion. Paul was the heftiest of the lot, and when I stood beside him, I looked tiny. He was contradictory to his physical appearance and was soft in his character. He would think twice before making any judgement.

We found one of those nice benches near the entrance of the canteen and chose to sit there. While Maahi, Priya and Paul chose to sit, Ajay and I were standing. All of a sudden, I felt a nudge from behind. And the next moment, the hot tea was on my shirt. It only felt a lot hotter.

I turned to look around who it was, and I saw a girl trying to gather books which had fallen down. I bent down to help her with the books to only figure out that it was Sakshi. She was surprised when she got to know it was me. Both of us got up on our feet in synergy.

"Rahul, I am very sorry," she said, looking into my eyes.

"I didn't mean it. I tripped at the steps," she added in an apologetic tone.

"Maybe the grudge is still on," I replied, and we burst out into laughter.

For the moment, I forgot the stain on my shirt, and I was looking at her eyes, as much as I could see myself into her eyes.

"So, we did meet again," she said.

Her voice broke my gaze.

"Yes, we did. Although this time I was not the one looking for you," I replied while dusting my clothes.

I remember the quote I once read:

When you want to meet someone, you will get to meet them someday.

I did finally meet her once again.

In the midst of the entire crowd around us, it felt that there were only the two of us. Every time I was looking into her eyes, it was getting difficult to take my eyes away. I wondered about what she would be thinking of me. My admiration for her was obvious.

I forgot the presence of my friends around me until Maahi tapped my back and gave me a wet tissue to wipe the stains.

"Hi, Sakshi," Maahi said, looking at Sakshi.

Maahi and Sakshi were regular to the sports complex and played badminton together.

"Hi, Maahi," Sakshi said. "Nice to meet you outside the complex."

Maahi gave me a glare from the corner of her eyes to let me know that she knew what I was doing at the badminton court the other day. I tried to avoid her glares.

"So, guys, must we leave now?" indicated Priya from behind. I did not bother to introduce my friends to her, not even as a courtesy.

I replied, "You guys carry on. I will catch you up at the class in a couple of minutes."

To my surprise, everyone left immediately without a fuss or taunt. I was pretty sure what I would face once I got back to the class. For the moment, I wanted to speak to Sakshi.

Hence, I stayed back as my friends left the place.

"So, what's up of late?" I asked her.

"Are you the boring professional type, Rahul?" she shot back.

Her reply was unexpected, but by now, I was getting used to her tone.

"It is with you, I am trying to show off," I replied with a touch of conceit.

"What a lie?" she replied.

"Yeah! Maybe I'll come up with a better reply the next time around," I said.

"Not impressive, yet again," she replied with a smile.

I kept wondering how she kept bulldozing me off in every conversation, and yet, I loved talking to her. I had to do something to change the topic of our conversation and hence got the focus back to sports.

"So, back to the court, is it?" I said, pointing towards the sports complex.

"Yeah, not the quitting type, I suppose," she replied, obviously a taunt. The taunt was not a one I liked, and I wanted to let her know that I too was a good enough badminton player.

"Good one. We should face off at the court someday. That should be fun," I replied with a grim.

"Do you play?" she asked.

"Everyone does one way or the other. Not sure, to which category I belong," I replied with some confidence.

I loved sports a lot, especially racquet sports. Badminton was a hobby for me, and I used to play it with my friends on a few evenings. Although I was not too bad at it, and I could at times surprise the best in the game, I would never claim myself to be a player. I would not claim that I play well with the ones who played for the college. I knew, on my day, I could run her close.

"How would I be assured that you wouldn't quit midway?" she asked.

I felt offended, and this was discomforting for me. I gave her a glare and replied in a serious tone, "Quitting is not my habit. It had to happen."

She could sense the disappointment in my tone, and softened her voice, and said, "You know what I feel?" she asked.

I looked at her, waiting for her to continue.

She took her bag, put it on her shoulders, and was about to walk away when she replied, "It was not your choice to quit. It was forced on you," and she left the place without speaking a word further. I could only look at her, in astonishment.

I stood there, seeing her walk away, and while she was almost out of my sight, I said, with a higher amplitude, "Sakshi, how did you know?"

She turned back, unleashed her dimple, at me and said, "You think only you can read my eyes."

Chapter Five

THE next time I met her was on the day when the results came out. I was sleeping at my house when the results came out. My father was trying to wake me up, and it wasn't easy. I had watched a couple of movies the previous night, and I had slept late.

"Your friends are already out there, and you are still sleeping."

Although his tone would seem like he was yelling at me, only I knew that he wasn't. In all these years, he had hardly scolded me. It was more of an extended friendship we carried apart from being a father and a son.

"They are out," said Paul, who barged right into my bedroom, early in the morning. He started shaking and waking me up, and I was too deep in my sleep, and it hardly mattered.

"I want to sleep a little while. Let us go later," I said, digging myself deeper into the quilt. It was strange that our college chose to display the results on the notice board rather than posting them online. Only after a couple of days, the results would be available online. We liked this tradition though. It gave us an opportunity to celebrate our happiness together.

Paul pulled me off my bed and forced me to get ready. In about thirty minutes we were at college. The results board were placed at the college reception. The sheet would have the roll number, followed by the names in alphabetical order and the GPA scores. Nearly ten students were around the board and a few near the steps leading to the college entrance. We were in no hurry, and we waited for everyone to leave. Once everyone left, Paul went to read out results. He scanned all the sheets, and read, "Ajay 9.4, Rahul 9.6, Maahi 8.9, Priya 8.79, Paul 8.6."

He turned around and looked at me in excitement and said, "Rahul, you have done it once again."

We were always the backbenchers of the class and would play some prank or the other in the class. We called ourselves the Pranksters. Despite all the pranks and the gaudy things we did in the class, and despite not being the favourites amongst the teachers, we consistently fared well in our exams. Our friendship was all about celebrating each other's successe. One amongst us would always take the pole position in the class. Twice it was me, and the other time it was Maahi. This time it happened to be my turn.

Soon, some of my classmates who had dropped by, walked up to congratulate me. Despite all the happiness and praises, I wanted to meet Sakshi more than ever before.

"Congrats, Rahul. Once again it's one of us," Priya said as she walked from behind. Getting marks and doing good in examinations was never on our minds, it happened. And whenever it happened, we used to feel happy and be proud.

"Let's celebrate," Maahi spluttered. It was her position that I took over. This semester, she had not performed as well as she is expected to, and yet she did not have any grudges about it. She was happy for me and wanted to celebrate.

"Okay. My treat at Polar Bear," I said and all agreed. Somehow, after every semester result, Polar Bear was a kind of hub where we went and had our favourite ice creams. Whoever was the topper amongst us would sponsor. We picked our bags, and as we were walking our way out of the college, Maahi stopped, looked at me and said, "Rahul, look who is there. Your girl!"

I wanted to shoot back, asking her whom she was referring to, but before I could, "What? Rahul's girl?" Priya asked.

"Who is that, Maahi?" Ajay remarked.

I was also curious about whom she was referring to. From the far off corner, I could see Sakshi, and I knew whom she was referring to. I looked at Maahi, and she smiled with a raised eyebrow.

Is this what you call telepathy? I wondered.

"Must I say, Rahul?" Maahi remarked.

For the moment, I was taken aback. I was confused about whether she was taking a guess or if she knew what I had in my mind. I had not shared with anyone how I felt when I see her. I tried to rebuke her and said, "Maahi, there is nothing of that sort. You better stay quiet."

She laughed once again at me, and it got the others curious as well. Each one of them started to scan in every direction, and I was hoping she did not come in our way.

"Wait, let me guess who it is," Priya said, scanning to see all the girls in her view. It did not take too much time as there were only a few of them, and finally, she said, "I got it."

"Me too," said Ajay, followed by Paul.

"What the hell is going on?" I screamed at them.

They all laughed at me and even booed. They did not let me speak a single word. Before I could even respond to them, everyone ceased to laugh, and Sakshi was right there in front of me.

"Hi, Rahul," Sakshi said.

Everyone around me kept quiet. They were watching us, albeit with a sly smile. I cleared my throat, trying to compose myself and said, "Hi."

She was wearing a pinkish top and light blue jeans. The morning wind was blowing her hairs, and her dimple was distracting me yet again. Her eyes, as always, were inviting. I wished to see, and there she was. And now, I was hesitant to talk to her, at least in front of my friends.

"So, what's up with your grades?" she asked, looking at me. For the first time, I was feeling good about my grades and felt proud about myself.

"Anything worthwhile mentioning?" she added.

"Yes. Before mine is your turn," I said with some confidence and pride.

"Slightly above average, 8.9," she said.

"And yours?" she asked.

By now, everyone's eyes were focused on me. My friends were keen on my reply. I had to sound modest. If not, my friends would fry me for their meals.

"9.6," I said in a modest tone. I had to try hard to not bring out my pride.

"Really?" her eyes lit up as she replied.

Before I could reply to her, Maahi shot up and said, "Yes, Sakshi. Can't you make out from the pride on his face?"

Sakshi's eyes turned towards Maahi for the first time. She had not seen her presence in the group.

"Hey, Maahi. Sorry, I did not see you."

"Why would you, Sakshi?" Maahi asked. And all of a sudden, all of us burst out into a laugh.

Sakshi had a sly smile on her face, and she looked at Maahi in an apologetic manner.

"Joining us at the Polar Bear?" Maahi asked Sakshi.

I gave a stare to Maahi, and everyone knew the reason for the invite. I knew my state if she happened to come, but yet, I was hoping that she came.

It took a couple of seconds for her to reply, "I have to leave now. You guys carry on."

She looked at me once again and congratulated me as we shook hands.

৵৽৽

Days went on and on, and our friendship grew like a house on fire. The days and times we met were always fun. We talked about each other's friends and the nasty things that happened during our childhood days. She spent a lot of time talking about her pet, Trashy, a little puppy dog. The time that we spent with each other was slowly getting longer.

We used to occasionally have our snacks together before we headed to our respective homes. I still remember the day I introduced her to my parents and the first reaction they gave.

"Isn't she too tall for you?" my dad exclaimed.

I was shocked by his response and Sakshi stood there confused.

And then my dad and mom broke down in laughter, and we all followed suit. It was all on a lighter note.

We loved playing a game of chess whenever we had the opportunity to do so. And every time, the loser had to do a task chosen by the winner. As a result of such tasks, I learned quite a few things she was good at, and a few things she was miserable with. I liked the fact that she loved music and was quite good at singing. And quite like me, she was pathetic at dancing.

I used to taunt her every time I made her dance and said, "Come on, you are showbiz."

And I loved to see her cute face when she was playfully angry.

The time I spent with my friends got lesser and lesser, but knowing them, they saw the funny side of it.

"You didn't have lunch with Sakshi?" they would ask. They knew that every single time they took her name, I would blush. And they would create a story out of it.

We maintained a candid conversation, especially when my friends were around. Both of us were quite aware of how focused my friends were on our conversation. I too enjoyed keeping my friends guessing about what was going on between Sakshi and me. Every single time, they asked me about it, I would reply, "We are just friends," and they would nod in disagreement.

Maahi used her friendship with both of us to her advantage. She would try to often invoke my name whenever she got a chance with Sakshi. Even while playing badminton, she would falsely praise me and see Sakshi's reaction. And then, the whole gang got a topic to talk about for the next time. I was the target of all these conversations.

"So they fried you for their lunch today as well?" Sakshi asked.

"How did you know that?" I asked her.

"Well, it's obvious, isn't it?" she replied with a smile.

"I am sorry if it hurts you," I said, pretending to be innocent.

"Shut up. I know you are having fun as well," she claimed.

"What do you mean by 'as well'?" I asked.

And I could see her biting her lips. They looked cute. Every little reaction she did now and then, made me want more.

"I meant your friends are having fun as well," she said with her eyebrows raised.

"My friends, which includes you as well. Isn't it?" And we both laughed.

Life was all about small moments like these. And I would want to thank my friends for providing them. They made our friendship turn into a beautiful bond. It felt like her beautiful soul was emerging out of its cocoon, and I was truly embracing it.

Chapter Six

A FEW weeks later, it was a bright Sunday morning, and we were driving to the Orchid's sports arena. Sakshi had a tournament at the Orchid's sport arena, and she asked me to come along. It was an offer I couldn't deny. I was waiting for such a moment.

I took half an hour to get ready, long enough for any man. I took my dad's car and informed him that I would need it the whole day. I passed by a flower shop and wondered if getting her a bouquet would be a good idea.

If I was going to propose her someday, I might as well start preparing for it now, I thought, smiling shyly at myself.

But then, I was not bold enough for it. And moreover, we have just got along, and I was not sure about her feelings about me.

Sakshi lived at a street in Defense Colony near Indiranagar. It was a posh locality with many trees. I felt like being in another country. There were entire families sitting on their porches with apparently nothing to do this Sunday morning than to watch me park my car.

I found some space in front of her house, looked at myself for one last time in the mirror and stepped into her house. The moment I opened the gate, the main door of her house opened, and Sakshi leapt out.

"Hey, Sakshi!" I heard one matronly type shout with great gusto.

"Hi, Aunty," I heard Sakshi bellow back.

"Who's the boy?" the aunty enquired in a subtle manner.

"He's my friend from my college," Sakshi called back.

It was an awkward moment, and she led me into her house.

I just stood there as Sakshi said, "This is my father."

Her father was about 5'9", which was slightly taller than me and was in his late fifties.

We shook hands, and he had a strong grip.

"How do you do, Sir?"

"Doing great," he replied with a very pleasant smile.

His smile was just the comfort I was looking for. One thing that helped me from my upbringing that day was about not talking with my mouth full.

"He is okay," said her father to his daughter.

What did that mean? I wondered.

"Well, you are in the third year, isn't it?"

He was now addressing me.

"Yes, Sir?"

Before he could go ahead with the conversation, Sakshi interrupted. "Shall we leave now? We are getting late."

I looked at Sakshi for conformance and nodded my head. I got up and shook his hand once again.

"Dad, we will leave now. I have placed your medicines on the table. Have your lunch and without forgetting, take them," she said, and both of us were walking towards the car.

"You are my daughter and not my mom. So don't you dare order me," he protested.

She turned around, paused near him, and gave him a warm little hug and both were smiling. I could see the admiration and love for one another in that little span of time.

We hit the roads before the traffic was up. Sakshi had occupied the co-passengers seat, and I was on the wheels.

"I had screwed up my preparatory board exams back then," I said.

It only took a glance for Sakshi to understand what I was talking about.

"It was not all my mistake. I had an off time. I kept losing matches and couldn't focus on studies as a result," I added.

"Isn't this common for a sportsperson in this country?" she said.

"True. He feared the worst for me. He concluded that I might not fare well in the matches I played, and neither would I fare well in my exams," I said.

She listened patiently without saying a word. That was the best thing about her. She knew when to speak and when to stay quiet.

"Someone had to come to me and instil some confidence. Someone had to believe in my abilities. As a seventeen-year-old, I didn't have it in me to prove the world wrong."

A little tear was trying to sneak its way out my eyes. She realized it and tapped my shoulder, trying to offer some comfort.

"You are someone who doesn't like to disappoint anyone, isn't it?" she asked.

"I am weak when it comes to fighting for my own cause. Moreover, being in a middle-class family and the only son, it was too much of a risk," I replied.

She couldn't have agreed more.

"How did you pick up the guitar?" she asked.

"It was Ramki. He is a musical geek. When we joined college, he inspired me into his guitar ambition. I was lured into his style."

But that's all. I didn't want to let the conversation drift into music and guitar. The drive, although inside the city, with traffic all around, still seemed to be the best I have ever had. I was already sharing things I had never done before, even to the best of my friends. Not that they didn't care, but we usually kept away from the sensitive topic.

There was silence in between, like in most of our conversations. And then, the bright sunshine started to look gloomy.

"I lost my mother when I was three. It is because of my dad that I am what I am today," she said in a softened tone.

"I have no siblings, and it was the two of us till date. He has done all that he could. He would not even raise his voice against me," she added.

Despite the sadness around her, she was never the emotional type. Maybe, she got it from her dad. She looked mature for her age. I let her speak, something I picked from her. I didn't have the urge in me to ask what had happened to her mother. Neither did I find it important to do so.

"My friends, some came in and left me. And some stayed along, but never so close," she said.

It was one of those moments where two hearts were sharing the deepest scars of their lives. Silence followed us, between every statement, but we knew we spoke to one another.

The drive led to us being comfortable with each other.

کچۍ

The Orchid's sports arena was looking stunning. They were beautifully lit, and the lights were beaming on the centre court. There were a couple of practice courts, which were occupied and Sakshi was playing a one-off match against a top club player. She loved participating in big tournaments, and since she did not belong to any particular club, she had to play a qualification match to prove her worth. Noah championships are usually played once every year. Players from all top clubs all over India take part in this tournament. Rankings to players are provided based on the past performance and as well as from the club performances. One needs to play qualification matches if they are not part of the top fifty rankings.

We both sat at the audience seat behind the courts. Her opponent was warming up in the practice court with her coach and Sakshi was looking at the two practices. I realized what was going on in her mind.

"Sakshi, can I see the racquet?"

She smiled and said, "Here you go."

She had a racquet bag, and inside it were four racquets and a few shuttles. I picked one of them and took off a shuttle.

"Come. Let's go," I said.

She picked her favourite racquet, and we walked to the second practice court.

I sent her a few knockdowns and was feeding a few to her backend. I winked my eyes whenever I got her to miss a few. Surely, she didn't expect this from me. We wrapped up the warm-up after about five minutes and soaked it in as the game was about to begin. Without any kind of realization or instinct, I hugged her just before the game was about to begin. She was taken aback by my gesture, but smiled and looked comfortable. To manage the situation, I said, "Just relax and play. Nothing to lose."

In a few minutes, the game began, and Sakshi seemed to be in a good frame of mind. She was clearly a lot more relaxed than the other day. She was moving very well and let her opponent do the running. The result was evident, and she wrapped up the game in style as the final scorecard read 21–10, 21–14.

Everyone at the court was stunned. This was not expected. I was the only one in the ground who congratulated her, and she had now qualified for the Noah championships. It was a dream come true for her. Yet, she was there, composed, showing no real emotions. She didn't even seem to be as happy as I was for her.

We got back into the car and closed the door. The moment I cranked the engine, she turned towards me and screamed, "Rahul, I won. Yeyyyyy."

She kept her happiness within the wraps to let it out when we were the two of us. I was surprised at her reaction.

"I owe this to you, and I wanted to let my happiness out only to you," she said.

And I shook my head and said, "You are crazy."

"I had played there a few times before. I used to walk in and walk out. No one cared," she said.

"And today, I wasn't alone, and I am no stranger to this place," she added and smiled.

Chapter Seven

IT was five-thirty in the morning, the next day, and I received a message from Sakshi.

Can you come to George Park now, please, if possible?

I was a little dizzy, but knowing Sakshi by now, I knew that there was something more important.

"Are you sure?" I replied.

Even before she could reply, I texted.

On my way!

It was one of those early winter mornings when you would believe the mist would wet your hairs entirely. I crossed the parade grounds, and while the roads were vacant, my mind could barely focus on them.

What the hell is she doing out there, so early in the morning? I wondered, and the very thought made me uncomfortable.

I sensed something was wrong. The very thought was disturbing, and I drove the car all the more faster. It took a few more minutes for me to be there.

❧❧❧

Her eyes were swollen. It looked as if she hadn't slept the whole night. There was a feeling of hatred. There was a feeling of fear.

She didn't know what had hit her hard. She seemed hurt. On seeing me, she cried further. She came closer to me and placed her head on my chest. It took a few long minutes before she could ease up. I let the moment pass by. But for sure, she would have heard my heartbeat rage faster.

Now she looked me into my eyes. I had never experienced such deep silence, and for so long.

"I am sorry to wake you up," she said. She cleared her throat and wiped her tears and said, "Your shirt is full of my tears," and managed a smile.

"Sakshi, don't be stupid," I replied.

"This is not for the first time I have come here this early." The tears once again started flowing out of her eyes, and she continued to speak.

I touched her arm and said, "Relax. Breathe first."

"Okay," she said. And I felt it could also mean, "I'll suffer through it."

I had no idea what she would be talking about. One thing was for sure, she was deeply hurt or scared of something, and she wanted someone to confide in.

"Somedays, I don't know why the scar of my life keeps haunting me all along, preventing me from sleeping," she said as I looked a little puzzled.

She turned away and looked in the direction of the sun.

"I cannot move on with my life," she continued.

"What is it, Sakshi?" I prodded her.

It took a couple of minutes for her to calm herself down and be stable. She pulled a water bottle from her car and sipped a little water till her throat felt a little better. She cleared her throat, splashed a little water on her face, and said, "I wish, I could change everything from my past."

She walked up to a bench and sat down, facing me.

"My mom was always my support back in those days. Her smiles, her encouragement, and she was always there for me."

A sob escaped her, and her shoulders started to shake, and she began to cry again. I walked up and sat beside her and held her hand.

"It was around eleven in the night. We were heading back home from a relative's wedding," Sakshi limped her voice throughout of her throat.

I held her hand even more firmly as she continued to speak.

"Everything was fine, and I fell asleep. But then I could feel the car steering towards its right harshly at a high speed."

She was inconsolable by now. I let her cry as much as she could.

"Before I could even open my eyes completely, I was blinded by the flash of headlights. I was not even given a chance to scream," she paused a bit and continued, "When I opened my eyes, I found myself in the hospital bed. I couldn't even move my legs and hands. The pain in my body was short-lived when the nurse told me that my mother had died in the accident."

A few minutes of silence followed as the passing breeze lightened the pain of her heart.

"You know, every now and then, I see this in my dream. Whenever my dad is in house, I go and lie down beside him. I have not said a single word about this to him," she said.

By now, the sun was in its full glory, and a lot more people were at the park.

"And whenever my dad is not around, I feel haunted at home. No matter what the time is, I would stroll down to this place. There is something special between me and this place. Today, somewhere there was an urge in my heart to be with you."

I smiled with assurance, and said, "The very fact that you shared all this with me itself is an indication of the trust you have in me. I will not break it for sure."

She looked straight into my eyes and said, "Rahul, you are very valuable to me. Us meeting each other may be an accident, but we being the friends we are is destiny. I can't take any other losses in my life. Promise me that no matter what, you will not ever desert me in my life."

Under the bright rising sun, I made the first promise of my life, and that was to last a lifetime.

Chapter Eight

I T was around 1 a.m in the morning when the beep of my phone woke me. I saw the message from Sakshi.

Are you awake?

My barely opening eyes lit up the moment I saw her name on the message. Sometimes, no matter how tired you are, and how sleepy you are, the moment you hear from someone you love, a fresh brand of energy flows within you. It was this energy that instantly got me up from my bed and made me sit for a conversation.

Not really.

I wanted to add, 'Was thinking about you', but refrained from doing so.

I know I am spoiling your sleep these days.

There were two meanings to that statement, and both of the meanings were true. I replied:

Lol. You do :)

For a good couple of minutes, there was no reply. I kept the phone aside and glanced at it now and then. I regretted sending the message now. I wanted to clarify my statement, but by then, the phone beeped again.

Oh, I am sorry. You carry on and have a good sleep.

I knew the intention behind her message. I typed and sent:

Ha-ha. I wish I could see your sad-looking face now.

She replied:

:-(

And I sent more smileys.

Time flew by, and we chatted all night long. This was the first time we conversed all night. For the next set of days, I slept at my class and stayed awake all night to chat with her. Every conversation we had in the next set of days was more about me exploring new stuff about myself. I could hardly believe what I was doing.

Even in those little naps, it was all about her. She was all around me, and my mind was always waiting for her. I wished to confess my love for her, now and then, but I dared not to. The most memorable days of my life were unveiling, and I did not want to spoil them.

Moreover, in all our conversations, we never let the topic drift away from the friendship zone. Both of us kept the relationship sane and drifted away from troubled waters. My day would start with picking her up from her house, and for this one reason, I wished for the sun to come up earlier.

Days came and went by, and one fine day, the urge in me got the better of me. A wave of courage stole me, and I wanted to confess my love for her. I was fairly confident about her feelings towards me. And it encouraged me further that day. All that I wanted was a moment and an opportunity.

God willing, he provided me with one as I received a message from her.

You know what? I have only a week left for the championship. I need you around me to train me for the next five days. Is this a game for you?

Why would I ever miss this opportunity? I wondered.

I replied:

Do you need to ask me that? Seriously?

She replied:

Well, I am being kind. You know I am, right.;-)

I replied with humour:

Who else apart from me? I still remember how kind you were when we met for the first time.

And as always, there was no reply for a few minutes after that.

Why is it that some girls take the lighter statements seriously and serious statements lightly? I kept asking myself.

Handling this part of her was always difficult for me, and it was very evident to her.

A few more minutes passed by, and I had to do damage control.

I texted:

Sorry. I didn't mean it. It was a joke.

A few minutes further paused, and by now, I was wondering if the problem was with the mobile network.

She replied:

Ha-ha. My dad called me and I was speaking with him.

And I felt embarrassed. I was the one who was overreacting.

ॐॐ

The tournament was over, and Sakshi was the runner up. Both of us were very happy, and we wanted to walk our way back home. In the blitz of the night, as the silence grew louder, the hiss of the train was occupying our ears. The silence was growing within our hearts, and perhaps the distance was shrinking along with it. As the train was nearing us, a few tired faces were pulling themselves up to get ready to board the train.

As the platform screen door of the metro train was opening, a little kid accompanying her parents getting off the train, looked at us and smiled.

We strolled into the train, but we chose to stand despite the empty seats around us. Our hands were firmly holding the grab rails, and we chose to use the same rail. They were closer to one another. The PSDs closed behind her, and I was facing her now. The still silence between us continued to grab our attention. If ever there was one pain, I would love to carry all along my life, it was this pain. The pain of silence while feeling her presence through my heart.

The train started with a whistle. The scenery outside was being unveiled as the train was slowing moving out of the railway station. The hustle and bustle of the city was turning into a vibrant darkness, and this darkness spread onto us as the train entered into a tunnel.

A tingle lingered over my heart when a ray of light spread onto her face like a little flash. It exposed the presence of a subtle smile on her face. This was the first time I was having a conversation without words. It brought out a smile to me.

I dared not to move an inch as I stood still. My heart was feeling the feast of every moment as the journey was sinking in. Stations came in and went, and so were the people. Every little time, the doors opened at the stations, a small little wind, now and then would let her hairs dance in joy.

I lived those moments, breathing a happy pain, with glances not lasting a second and a bit beyond. It took, maybe, a little longer than twenty minutes, which was seemingly a time worth a life for her to look at me again. I wished she did not look at me as I loved the feeling of being in pain.

Then came that little expression on her face, filled with painstaking demure. It was worth a skip of the beat. It was as if someone was mesmerizing me and letting my heart dance to their tunes. Nothing could have probably woken me out of that enigma, but for her smile that followed. I froze deeper.

This smile was the beginning of cataclysm within my heart, which would never end within me. In the starkness of the movement, my love for her brimmed along my soul.

Without saying, I knew what was going on in her heart. The scent of the moment was keeping us in the same place harmoniously for a while. Crazily though, I wished I could prevent my eyes from blinking. She looked at me only to gift me a smile, and with a little flair, would instantly turn back to staring at the door behind me.

It was the gracefulness of the moment that led me into believing that even a word spoken would break the mist. I was failing to garner enough strength in my throat to spell out even a few words. Not for the first time, that day, I felt that she was gorgeous. That image of her is engraved on my heart forever.

Like every beautiful journey, this too had to come to a halt. The stereophonic sound of the station name could not play a perfect spoilsport. It was then that we woke out of our isolated world. As the PSDs opened, the fresh breeze of night air welcomed us. We walked out or rather strolled out. Maybe the same tune was flowing in our hearts, which led us to walk in harmony as we just heard the sound of our footsteps.

The breeze was getting stronger and colder as we walked onto a well-lit deserted street. I wished I could get down on to my knees and tell her how I truly felt for her. I wanted to talk a lot to her, about the beauties of my life, but none was worth a mention in front of her. The rhyme in my heart was playing a lullaby that was strong enough to keep my throat asleep. It would not say a word.

My heartbeats were racing against time as we were approaching her house. The anxiety of not having said what I wished to tell her was growing all along. Our footsteps grew shorter and were longing to walk longer. Freezing of time was not within our control, but then we could freeze this moment of ours.

I stood as she walked ahead, only to turn back and look at me. I grabbed my phone out of my pocket and looked at her. She smiled and walked further ahead. I smiled and leapt ahead a few steps to catch up with her, and we stood. I raised my hand and placed the camera of the phone focusing our faces and the silent road behind us. She smiled, and so did I as I captured a long-lasting frame, which can never be erased from my memory.

As we continued to walk, the street lights turned off. We were left with the company of the moonlight. Soft as it could ever be, the faded out, milky light was easing out the feelings within us. Was it the photo, the moonlight, or the cool breeze which made me feel lighter and different? I felt that I was breathing again after a while. We were a few steps closer to her house. Having not spoken to her for a while now, I was longing to hear her voice. The anxiety of having to travel back in loneliness was brewing inside me. I wished I heard something from her today. We were only a few steps away from the gate of her house. She paused, turned around and looked back at me, waiting for me to say something.

The courage that I thought was within me at the start of the day fell flat in front of her. All that I could muster out of me was a smile, and she smiled back, nodded her head and said, "Bye."

Chapter Nine

SOME things in life are more beautiful when not told, but experienced. That was exactly the way I felt the next few months. If a single word could describe our daily life in those months, it is 'prodigious'. Every waking moment was about focusing on what new we would do that day.

The game of cat and mouse continued between the two of us on who would say the obvious first. Usually, it was even. Despite it, we managed to construct the most memorable and beautiful moments of my life. The moments that I would love to savour all my life and the moments I would wish to re-live every single day.

Life changes and good things don't last forever. The first brink of destiny stuck when I finished my final year exam. I found a job at Steve's Inc, a multinational company at Chennai. I had pretty much made up my mind on the last day of college to confess my feelings to Sakshi about her.

Although I was very well aware that it was not going to be the last day I would be meeting her, on that particular day, I felt a strong vibe within me to spell it out. The fear of missing her friendship had outweighed all the other possibilities until then, which was the reason I deprived myself of numerous opportunities to express my feelings.

We met at the entrance of the college, and we decided to spend some alone time with one last walk around the campus. We walked past our college library and were heading towards the badminton court. My heart was pounding harder, and I sincerely wished I had more courage to express my love to her. The words were failing to fall in place, and it was getting a lot nervier.

"The badminton court, you will not be around when I play here again," she said, looking at the badminton court.

Silence followed, and now, a tear appeared at the corner of her eyes.

"You were the only one I had, Rahul," she said as her emotions started to flow out.

In nearly the two years with her, patience and active listening was something I had developed.

"The last two years you were there, almost always, and I never realized that time existed and today... I have this strange feeling of you walking out of my life forever."

She stopped walking and looked at my eyes, and tears started pouring out of her. I desperately wanted to hug her and say, "I will not leave you forever, and I want to spend the rest of my life with you."

She could sense the discomfort in me, but then I managed something I had not done in the last two years.

I lifted her hand and held it closer to my heart, and said, "I promise you I will never let you feel lonely, no matter where I go."

She could sense the truth in my eyes. The words were coming out of my heart.

"I had promised you earlier, and today again, I say the same thing."

I looked into her eyes, and said, "Nothing will change, Sakshi. Nothing."

The sound of thunder helped us to shrug off that moment, and we continued our walk.

Somewhere in those moments, I felt the longingness in her to have a companion in her life. Someone whom she could trust and rely on at all times.

"I cannot afford to miss you in my life, Rahul," she said as we kept walking. "You know me very well, and you are someone I can look to when in need."

My mind was clouded with a lot of thoughts and emotions now. I decided not to express my feelings for her during this time. She trusts me, and when she was down, it was not the right time for me to discuss something complicated. Moreover, I did not want to shatter her further.

"Trust me, and I am always present for you," I assured her again.

A quiet walk followed until we were joined by Maahi.

"Everyone is waiting for you. A group pic," Maahi said.

"I am really sorry for that," I replied.

"Don't be. You must have been caught up with something really important," Maahi said as she winked.

I smiled and ignored the last statement as we walked up to join the rest of the group.

"I will be back in a few minutes," I said to Sakshi, and she nodded her head.

While the photographs were being taken, at a far distance, I could see Sakshi vanishing off my radar into the crowd.

ॐॐ

There were a couple of weeks between college exams and the date of joining Steve's Inc. Although she didn't like it, I picked her up from her house every single day and dropped her back. By now, her dad knew me well, and whenever we got an opportunity, we used to converse for long hours. We had different views on various topics like politics and cricket. But that was what probably made us get along so well. We always agreed to disagree.

There are times when you do not know the zone your friendship is with a person. This was true, between Sakshi and me. And I kept wondering what her dad thought about us. Was he so cool with me because he only considered me to be a friend to her? What if he knew that I loved her? Would he be the same? Would I end up breaking his trust?

Lots of questions kept disturbing me. Waiting and letting it go with the flow was the only thing I could do at best.

She was always busy the whole day with her classes, and all I did was wait for the time we could be together. I was not as keen on meeting my other friends during this time. No matter with whom I was, I always felt the longing-ness for her.

The best part of my relationship with Sakshi was that we never let each other intrude into the other's time and space. We had unwritten regulations, and we stuck to them. It could also be our understanding of one another that made it possible. She knew I would wait for her all day. And she ensured that the time she was with me was whole and solely for me. She let no distractions come in between. I too ensured that despite my loneliness, I would not disturb her while she was busy. She kept her badminton and academics undisturbed.

"Seven more days," she would say. She kept reminding me about my joining date. We very well knew that the day of my departure was nearing, but then we had no solution. Life had to move on.

To a large extent, both of us avoided talking about it. Being connected on the mobile was the only way to stay in touch. But then talking about it was only going to stress us and lead us into a depression. Hence we confined ourselves to the present.

We knew that WhatsApp and Skype would keep us close despite the distance. The feeling of going away from her kept the happiness in having found a good job away. There were five of us from the college who had offers from Steve's Inc. Every time we met, they seemed too excited. The talks inside this gang always revolved around the new job and what we must do in Chennai. A WhatsApp group was formed and the plans on how we spent our weekends and what all we should do for the next year was already set in place. In most of these conversations, I was a mute spectator.

My friends would always mock me for the face I used to put up during such conversations. At times, with so many companies in Bangalore, I wished I could find a job here itself. Some things always don't go the way we want it to. To be fair to myself, there was a part of me that was happy to go to a new place and to be part of such a big and proud organization.

Chapter Ten

IT was my first day at the office, and I along with a group of new joinees were sitting in a conference room along with the HR. All five of us joined the same office. This for the first time I was no longer a student. We were referred to as engineers by the HR team. It gave me a strange feeling. The feeling of being an employee and the happiness surrounding it was overweighing the pain of not being a student.

The first day was about filling a lot of documents, which was tiresome. At the same time, we had a lot of excitement. There were lots of new people around from different colleges and with different backgrounds. We were told that there were about eighty new joinees that day and each one would be placed at a different location and in different teams.

It took a while for the ice to be broken, and once it was done, there was no stopping. We utilized a lot of the available free time to chitchat and get to know each other. Each one of us felt good to know about each other and be part of such a big organization. For the first few months, it was more like a college environment. The coffee breaks and lunchtime were meant fun. Each one of us met during this time.

Topics had no limits for us, and we preferred to talk about our college experiences. Our office pantry had a subtle feel to it with new lights and was intended to encourage collaboration.

It had a refrigerator, a coffee vending machine and storage places for cutleries. There were a few seating chairs and small coffee tables to people to sit and sip their favourite coffee. During the first few days, our batchmates kept ensuring that we occupied those seats on a frequent basis.

It took a few days for me to be assigned to a project. People came into my life, one after another, and I was no longer in control of what was happening around me. The amount of time I was spending with any of my college friends was shrinking day by day.

For the first few days, there were lots of training sessions, a few of them were boring. And the others, were there to make us feel as if we did not belong here. Our time was split into attending classroom-training sessions, coffee breaks or lunch. It all seemed perfect, and I was enjoying my time at the office. At the same time, during the weekends, I was able to catch up with Sakshi and my other friends on the mobile. Good things and a balanced way of living did not last for long. The first stroke of reality stuck when my team leader, Gaurav, walked up to me.

When I think of Gaurav, I could remember his sarcastic looks and his masculine beard. He was loud, and an extremely proud person, which used to make him go overboard many times. He commanded respect from his subordinates and was leading a team of ten engineers, including me. There is something about managers and how much they loved carrying their laptops and headphones along with them at all times, which I have never understood.

He once saw me taking a long time during my coffee break and came up to me, and said, "Enough of having fun, Rahul."

His looks were intimidating. During those days, I felt that my entire future was dependent on him. He always gave me the impression that if I screwed up my work, my job was gone. This happened to be the first bite of my corporate journey. We had to pretend like we were working all day, even if we had no work. Whenever I found a little space and time in my cubicle, I used to chat with Sakshi.

One day, he called me and a few of my other colleagues, Vicky and Armaan, to a meeting. There was silence as Gaurav switched on his Apple Mac Book as he placed himself on the sofa.

"Okay then," Gaurav said. "I guess we should start our meeting now."

"Of course," Vicky said.

This was my first formal meeting with him, and I could sense some uneasiness within me.

"So, Rahul, how have the last few months been?" asked Armaan.

"They were okay. I got good training and know the concepts well," I replied.

Armaan looked at me and asked again, "Are you sure?"

And I nodded.

"Okay, so there is this task that we need you to start working on," Gaurav said.

I looked at him with eagerness.

Finally, some work, I thought.

Everyone's first assignment is a milestone in their careers. This was the moment I was waiting to hear for months. My first chance to prove to myself that I could indeed work in such an organization was right there.

Gaurav and Armaan took a couple of minutes to explain what needed had to be done. After asking them for a few clarifications, I said, "Sure, I will start working on this."

The sarcastic smile brimmed up on me once again, as if to say, 'really'?

"The deadline is two weeks from now," Armaan said.

Now, my voice was slurred, and I felt it was asking a lot out of me. Saying 'no, it cannot be met', was not going to be taken in the right spirit as this was my first assignment. I had to accept the timeline and do it. I had never felt so vulnerable before.

"Are you sure?" I said, trying to give myself a second chance.

"Yes," Armaan said and walked away towards his desk.

He did not even care to wait long enough for my nod. It seemed like a ghost was creeping on to me and tapping my shoulder. Everyone dispersed, and I stood there, clueless.

I organized a few finer details about the assignment. I had to ensure that none of the details provided to me during the briefing was lost.

The very next thing, I did was to walk up to my batch mates and discuss with them about the assignment.

"Hold on, man. Take it easy," a soft voice from behind me comforted me.

From the voice, I could make out that it was of Sushma. She was my senior in college and a couple of years older to me. I had known her since my college days as she used to travel in the same college bus as me.

"I will help you with that," she said to me and led the way to her desk.

I pulled a chair from other cubicle and sat beside her.

"So what is the task about?" she asked.

I spent the next few minutes explaining to her the task and the expectations from Gaurav. She waited, watched and listened to me until I completed. She then broke down the whole thing into granular details to make it look easy.

This was my first experience on how to break down complicated stuff to arrive at much simpler steps to reach my goal. Once I figured out what needed to be done, my energy and excitement was all back again. I worked for long hours. I used to be in the office on all days including weekends. Every single achievement I had during this phase felt sweet. The pride within me and the sense of accomplishment was immense. And in two weeks' time, I stood there, pulling my moustache, glancing at Gaurav.

His sarcastic and intimidating looks no longer bothered me, and I was confident about facing him today. I knew I had made my mark.

Chapter Eleven

THE work increased day by day, and I was getting addicted to my work. I was indeed performing well in the organization. Work was getting me to me, and my mind was always thinking about other tasks and problems. Every minute I was awake, and at times, even during my sleep, it was chasing me.

By the time I got back home every single day, I was so exhausted that I preferred to skip my dinner. Messaging and reading messages were the last things on my mind. Every single time Sakshi messaged me, I was answering back objectively.

Our conversations, which used to last forever, were now getting shorter day by day. It was not going beyond five messages. Most of the weekends were spent in the office and on the rest of the weekends, I preferred to stay indoors. Being in the software industry was getting stressful and my mind and body needed longer breaks. Every single time Sakshi wanted to meet me and asked me to travel to Bangalore, I was giving one reason or the other.

It was a pity that, at times, Sakshi used to stay awake on the days I was returning back late from the office so that she could chat with me for a while. And I would be so exhausted that within two messages of chatting, I would say:

I have to sleep now. Let us chat tomorrow.

I knew very well that I was not keeping my promise I gave her, but then this was not how I expected my work to be. My life had changed, and I was getting more associated with my friends from the office. This was due to their understanding of what I was going through. Within three months, my excitement with work and the software industry went out, and by now, I was like a machine with no heart.

They always say that the software industry is a place which changes you as a person. I was always confident that I wouldn't change, but without my knowledge, I too ended in the cattle.

It was Saturday, early in the morning around 7 a.m, I received a call from Sakshi. I was deep in sleep as I had returned from the office only at 2 a.m. I had to make an important bug-fix release on that day. I heard the call, but then I chose to ignore it. She called me about three times, and I couldn't convince myself to wake up from bed. In a few seconds, there was a beep, and yet, I made no effort to check my phone.

I was back asleep again, and I woke up at around 11 a.m. By the time I woke up, I was very hungry, and I grabbed a few pieces of bread and made an omelette. The calls in the morning were completely out of my mind. Only after I finished my breakfast and bath, I remembered the calls from Sakshi in the morning. I took my phone and had a look at the messages. There were about seven calls and twelve WhatsApp messages.

The WhatsApp messages read…

7:15 AM   : Can you call me. It is urgent.

7:25 A.M : I need your help. Please call me.

7:27 A.M : Missed call from Sakshi.

7:31 A.M : Call me now. Dad is not well.

7:33 A.M : I need to take him to hospital. Leaving now.

8:12 A.M : Missed call from Sakshi.

8:15 A.M : Missed call from Sakshi.

8:20 A.M : This is serious. Please call me or else I won't speak to you.

8:30 A.M : Missed call from Sakshi.

9:00 A.M : You don't value me or care for me.

9:01 A.M : I don't need you anymore.

9:02 A.M : Thanks for all that you have done. I can handle myself.

9:10 A.M : Missed call from Sakshi.

10:00 A.M : Missed call from Sakshi.

10:10 A.M : Missed call from Sakshi.

10:32 A.M : You have killed me from the inside today.

10:32 A.M : I was a fool to trust you.

10:33 A.M : Live your life and don't ever call or message me again.

10:33 A.M : Thanks and goodbye.

I did not know how to react when I read her messages. It was all grey for me. My mind was going blank and was also feeling guilty for not picking her call when I could have. I had to face it, and I decided to call her immediately. After a couple of rings and she picked the call.

"Hi…" she said.

There was grief and anger in her tone.

"Sorry, I had come late in the night and slept off," I replied hesitatingly.

There was a pause from her side, and she replied, "Sorry for disturbing you during your sleep."

It was a direct jab at me, and it didn't feel good. I could understand her emotions behind the statements.

"How is your dad now?"

"Heart attack in the morning, and now out of danger," she said with tears and determination in her voice.

I was in a state of shock. He was all good when I met him the last time. He was very health conscious. Whenever I met him in person, on the days when Sakshi was around, he used to talk about his fears. He feared for her. He talked to me about how lonely she would be if something happened to him. I could recollect one particular statement of his.

"Rahul, I am glad Sakshi found you. I trust you to be with her all through her life." He had broken down when he said this to me.

"What are you saying, Sakshi?" I was yelling in shock.

She was incredibly stable the next moment, and she said, "I wouldn't vouch a lie on him. You know that."

"When did this happen?"

"I saw him struggling for breath in the morning. That's when I called you," she said.

"Sorry to hear that and sorry that I did not pick up the call."

"No problem. It doesn't matter now. The ambulance was on time. Thankfully. If not..." and she started to cry.

She kept sobbing, and that is all I could hear for the next few minutes.

"There was no one, and I wanted you to be around," she said.

I could sense the pain in her voice, and I had no clue about how to calm her. I was worthy enough to take the blame.

"I will join you there by tonight. I will leave immediately."

She didn't expect that reply from me, but her tone sounded better thereafter.

"No, it's okay. He is good now, and I have asked my friend to come over," she said.

"It is not about you, Sakshi. It is about me, and I want to be there with you. And moreover, it is for your dad as well," I shot back.

A smile seemed to have emerged from her, and she replied, "I am glad you said that, Rahul. But it is fine for me, and, I don't want to build high expectations and be a trouble for you."

I knew that despite her statements, she wanted me to be with her. Her loneliness during such a moment was hurting her, and she needed a let out. For the last two and a half years, I was the only person who was with her during her happy and sad moments, and today I had deserted her. I did not want to let her down further, and I said, "I promise that I will be coming tonight. Stay relaxed."

It took a few minutes for me to convince her, and finally, she said, "I will be waiting for you. Don't let me down again please."

൹

A few minutes later, I packed my bags and was looking for flights between Bangalore to Chennai. The earliest flight was at 6:30 p.m. This was pretty late as it would reach Bangalore around 7:30 p.m and then from Bangalore Airport to the hospital would take about 1 and a half hours, which would mean I would not reach before 9 p.m. There was a train leaving Chennai at about 1 p.m, and I wanted to take it. That gave me a chance to be there at around 8 p.m. I took a taxi to the railway station. While I was on the way, I got a call from Sushma.

"The code broke, Rahul," she said. This was least expected.

"But I had tested it very well," I replied.

"It happens, Rahul. Gaurav wants the release by Monday morning. The testers are there tomorrow. So the fix should be given by tonight."

I was clueless and had no idea what to do. I knew how important the release was for the organization. The product launch was around the corner, and as always, there was already a lot of hype in the media about the product we were developing. A small glitch during the press release event and subsequent user demo sessions would result in bad reviews for the product. There were quite a lot of competitors in the market for this product segment.

We were the first ones to go for a launch and any delay in the launch would jeopardize the company's image.

"Rahul, we cannot release it without solving this bug. It will be noticed immediately," Sushma said.

"But, Sushma, I am on my way to Bangalore due to some emergency. Can you handle it?" I asked hesitatingly.

"It is your code, and you know it better. Gaurav will not let me touch it, especially at this time. So it is better you come," she insisted.

"I do have to go Sushma. It is important."

We were pondering for options, and after a while, she said, "I guess it should be easy for you to fix it. I will join you at the office, and once you fix it, you can leave immediately. I will take care of the rest."

It sounded reasonable. It gave me a chance to take the 6:30 p.m flight if I could fix the issues by then.

I reached office at around 2 p.m and was taken aback when I saw the whole team. A couple of people who were missing were on their way as well. The whole team was called in order to ensure that issues found at the last minute by the testing team could be fixed and released immediately. The management had laid a rule that no one was to leave until the testing team completed a full cycle of tests and found no issues and the software was qualified for release.

It was my first experience of a product release. A war room setup was created wherein the developers involved in bug fixing a particular issue were held up in a room along with the managers, and all decisions and fixes were reviewed instantly and tested.

I was inside the war room as it was the bug from my code which was identified as a show stopper for the release. Apart from mine, there were a couple of other bugs identified as show stoppers. Sushma accompanied me to the war room.

We started to work on the issue, and in a few minutes, I was sucked into the environment. All my focus turned towards solving the issue, and I completely forgot about Sakshi. It took us nearly three hours to provide a fix to the issues. We were not allowed to leave the room, and we were asked to wait until the code review and testing was completed.

Food was ordered for the entire team and was provided to us inside the office itself. Each one of us took turns to have our food, and we had to be back to our places as soon as we could. It took an hour for the testing and code review to be complete, and to my horror, the fix failed in a different use case scenario.

I can still remember the look on Gaurav's face when the testing team gave us a thumbs down. It made me feel like I had committed the biggest crime on earth, and I would be crucified immediately.

Another four hours for fixing the issue and two hours for test and review followed, and it cost me ten long hours for getting the go-ahead for my release. During this whole time, I was not allowed to use my phone, and the phone charge was down as well. I left the war room, and I went back to my desk. I had to wait for about ten hours until all the other issues were fixed and the final software release was confirmed.

My mind was so stressed out during this phase, I almost slept at my desk in the office. All that I could think have now was, sleep and sleep.

It was only on the next day that I came back home, and I put my phone back to charge. I had no clue on how I would convince Sakshi. She must have lost her hope in me. I did not have the guts to call her up. The only thing that occurred to me was to take a quick nap and then leave to Bangalore soon after.

Chapter Twelve

I REACHED the hospital the next morning and found Sakshi sitting at the waiter lounge all alone.

"I need to talk to you."

"What's there to talk to me?" she replied.

"I understand that you are mad at me."

"Do I look mad?"

"Not only do you look mad, but you sound that way too," I said, staring at her.

"But why do you bother?"

I could sense the feeling the crackle of tension between us.

"I am sorry I couldn't keep my words."

"Tell me something new," she replied.

"I do deserve a chance to provide an explanation."

"Of course, you do, but it won't change my feelings."

"I had already left my home to come to Bangalore, but then I got a call to come to the office. I had to go Sakshi."

"Yes, work is important. And your mobile got switched off, isn't it?" she murmured.

"Yes, unfortunately."

"And you didn't have other means to inform me, right?"

I kept quiet for a while and said, "I have no answers to your questions. It was the situation, and I believe there is no fault of mine in this. I did all that I could."

The situation was too surreal to absorb. I held my head in disbelief and resisted any further words.

The frustration was clear from her expressions as she shook her head to disagree with all that I had to say. All this was followed with a few minutes of silence.

"Why aren't you saying anything?" I asked.

"It is because I am scared."

"Scared? Scared of what?"

Tears started flowing from her eyes, and she took a couple of seconds to steady herself. In a very controlled and subtle tone, she put up a very brave face, took a deep breath, and said, "Scared of myself. I had realized the pain of being dependent on people, and today, you have injected it once again on me."

"What do you mean by that?" I shot back.

"The trust is broken, Rahul. The deepest of my pains are known to you, only you. And when I looked at you for comfort, you have instead injected more."

A wave of emotions was flowing within me, and it was oscillating between trying to stay calm one moment to extreme anger in the next.

"Listen, I am sorry. I should have informed you. And I know very well about what you have gone through. It was my situation and…"

And by the time I finished saying the statement, she interrupted, "It is not about you, Rahul. It is about me. I don't want to blame you. It was my fault to have trusted you. If you had not offered to come at all, I wouldn't have been hurt as much as I am now."

Once again, silence descended. Albeit the anger was not embedded in her tone, it was visible in her words.

"Between all this, when I couldn't reach you for so long, I was worried. I wondered if something had gone wrong with you on the way. Thirty-six hours and no call from you. Do you even know how many times I have tried to reach you? What all should I be worried of?"

Her voice was getting stronger every moment, and her pain was flowing out of her by now. She was inflicting them back to me. I was struggling to find ways to calm her down. I pulled myself closer to her, and in an apologetic tone, I said, "Give me one more chance please?"

She gave a sarcastic look and said, "One more chance… my life, my emotions, my stress and my dad. I can't risk another chance."

The storm, the pressure and the stress between the two of us was real. I had never faced something like this before. All the while, during my journey, I was preparing for something like this. But, by now, I realized that no matter how much the preparation, I was not ready to face this.

My shoulders dropped down in resignation, and each moment was getting more difficult than the last. I wished I could run to her and hug her.

"There is a lot of satisfaction when you know someone likes you and cares for you. You gave me that satisfaction a lot of times, Rahul," she said as she leaned towards a wall.

"But, I am getting weaker, all the more in your company. My mind is getting stressed floating between trust and hopelessness. I cannot take this more. I am done, Rahul," she said.

"You don't want to consider my point of view and how helpless I was, is it?"

"Again, it is not about you, Rahul. It is about how dependent I was on you and how nervy I felt when you were not around, and I couldn't reach you."

I stood there and was already expecting the worst from her.

"Right now, I want to take good care of my dad. This is my priority and focus. Let us drift apart in our own paths, Rahul. Without any more hurt, guilt and every other thing, I need peace. I will not trouble you anymore and do not want to hear from you as well."

I nodded my head, looked away and I tried to garner some strength in my mind.

She saw for one last time, into my eyes, and said, "Thanks again for all that you have been in my life. Goodbye." And she walked away.

Her words sounded real, and her pain was immense. Anymore words that I would speak would have broken her further, and I did not want to inflict more pain.

Strange, as it may sound, we had a breakup, even before confessing our love to each other.

Chapter Thirteen

A WAIT is always endless. Time flies, people move on, but the hope stays. I waited and waited for her to get back to me. Stuck in a horizon where waiting was my only hope, I could hardly concentrate on my work. Days went along, and the purpose of waiting was getting away from me.

I kept venturing into newer pastures to distract my mind away, but nothing lasted for too long. I kept asking myself if keeping away was the right thing to do. I had to respect her words, and I did that.

It took me three long years until I accidentally came across my college photos. They were stored on my iPhone, and I decided to re-ignite all those memories. I ran through them, starting in reverse chronological order, from present to past. The majority of the photos were with my office friends, involving the lunch outings, team building activities and us hanging out at various coffee shops. They made me feel good.

As I was ambling on, the photo of Sakshi and me, which we took on our night walk, popped in front of me. The smile on my face departed, and a feeling of sorrow smudged into me. I felt alone and silent. I zoomed into the photo to see her smiling face. I saw my face on the photo, and then I saw my face in the mirror. What I was missing was truly evident. The smile in the photo was a measure of true happiness. I knew what I was missing in my life.

The next couple of minutes passed without me taking my eyes off that photo. Life was not about office and work, but they are moments. To be with someone whom you love and who loves you means a lot more than anything else. I closed my eyes, and I saw her image, still lingering in my heart. I could see her face when she left me. They were sad and perhaps wanted to say something, which I failed to understand until now.

What happened to her dad that day?

Why was she so upset?

Is it possible for someone to keep away for so long?

I was pondering over a lot of questions. What if there was a bigger problem which she was hiding from me?

In life, sometimes you would want to give yourself a second chance. People have changed over time, and time doesn't wait for anyone. The feeling of letting her go for all my life was itself painful. In no time, I found myself sitting on the train from Chennai to Bangalore.

ॐॐ

The initial days after parting ways with her was always about blaming her for not understanding my situation in the office. I felt that she had unrealistic expectations of me.

Today, when I look back, I could understand how it was to be alone. After getting obsessed with someone's company, it is very hard to stay alone. She was someone who had very little friends. I was more like a puppy to her, caring and being with her always.

Perhaps, I could have cared for her more. I could have spent a lot more time on her. I could have visited her more often. Lots of things I could have done. It was not all about friendship, it was way beyond that. I was partly culpable for her situation.

I had this habit of forecasting and role-playing certain situations that could happen. I had to be prepared for them beforehand.

What if she was not in town? I thought.

I would only have to return back disappointed. Maahi was the only one who could have remotely known about her. I decided to call Maahi to check if Sakshi was in town.

"Hey, how surprising?" Maahi said as soon as she picked up my call.

"On my way to Bangalore. So needed information."

"No wonder. Tell me."

"Do you have an idea about Sakshi? Is she in town?"

Maahi stayed silent for a few minutes.

"I am not sure. Maybe not." Her voice sounded hesitant.

"Is there something wrong, Maahi?" I asked briskly.

"Nothing, Rahul. Why do you ask about her?"

I was not sure if I wanted to express my interest in meeting Sakshi to Maahi. I chose not.

"Just like that, I asked."

"The last thing I heard about her was about two years ago. She doesn't come for badminton anymore."

I stayed silent. I started to wonder if I was the cause for all this.

"Rahul, it's not you. Don't worry, pal," Maahi said as she understood what would be going on in my mind.

"It is because of me," I said honestly.

"Shut up and don't take all the blame onto yourself."

"It is not blame, but the truth."

We kept arguing on the topic for a few minutes until she said in the heat of the moment, "Aryan is with her these days."

I did not know how to react, and I couldn't believe what I just heard. All that I could say was, "Okay. Thanks, Maahi. I will call you later."

I dropped the call and was processing the information from Maahi. Suddenly lots of confusion popped up in my mind.

"Would it be true?"

I kept asking myself all along. I knew Maahi, and I knew Sakshi even better. The place that Sakshi gave me in her life can't be taken by anyone else. But then, she had never confessed her love for me. We had been hopping on the thin line between love and friendship.

"Did I lose her already?"

It was my mistake, and I had to set it right. No matter what, I wanted to apologize to her for behaving the way I did. It was a different kind of feeling in me, and I was feeling guilty. There was something wrong that day, and I should have heard her side of the story.

I felt a quick shiver in my spine as I wondered, What if I happened to see her with Aryan?

How would I even face her?

How would I talk to her?

What happened to her in these three years that she did not get in touch with me?

All sorts of questions was bothering me. I felt I would look like a stranger in her eyes now. Yet, I did not want to close my heart once again. There WAs a part of my heart, a big one, which was still in love with her and would always be. This time it was not willing to give in, yet.

I had a couple of choices. The first was to continue with the flow, by shutting off my heart and going back. The second was to trust her and go ahead in the search of my love.

During the times when I am confused, I let my heart make the decisions. I felt that this was probably my last choice to be a part of her life. Maybe it was already late, but I had no choice.

Chapter Fourteen

SEEING someone who you loved so deeply after three years is so crazy and exciting that you forget where you are. I spent thinking the next half an hour or so thinking about how she would react on seeing me. 'What-if' she did not want to see me. All these kind of thoughts were inside me.

For the next half an hour or so, I sat at my favourite restaurant at M.G Road, wondering how I would approach this. The time I took to eat my meal seemed much longer than the travel time from Chennai to Bangalore. Should I message her, enquiring about where she is or should I go directly to her house? Clarity struck me after a few minutes when I finally convinced myself that meeting her was the best way. I could get what she felt by looking into her eyes for what she felt.

After lunch, I took a cab to her house at Indiranagar, which was about a fifteen minute drive. The music was beating inside my ears from my headphones, helping me to lower my anxiety levels. It did its job quite a bit, but my anxiety remained. Staying still inside the cab itself was a big task.

Fifteen minutes later, after sneaking past the traffic, I was there, at 2 p.m in the afternoon in front of her house.

The paint of her house gate had gone pale, and the leaves of the sole tree that stood beside the house compound was littered all over the place. Lots of dust had accumulated on the lamp in front of her house, and it looked like a house that was almost abandoned. The guava tree that once gave a lot of tasty fruits seemed to have dried out as I could only spot a few. Somewhere within me, there was a feeling that no one was living in the house.

I checked if the gates were locked, and no, they were not.

I heard a creaky noise from the gates as I tried to open them. The car, usually parked in front of her house was not there. It was a Renault Duster, and her father used to be very proud of it. I garnered a few leaps of courage to walk ahead and rang the bell.

Those few minutes that I stood there was when I heard my heartbeat clearly. All that was flowing in my mind was about how she would react on seeing me. My confidence to face her stood broken, and a layer of guilt was settling on me. It was my mistake to have ignored her for this while. It was me who had not picked her calls. I wanted to leave without seeing her, but then my feet were not giving up and were taking me towards the door.

A nervous shiver of my hand followed when I rang the calling bell in front of the main door. A few seconds there, and there was just silence. I was hoping that no one would open the door. A few more seconds followed, and the silence was disturbed by the sound of the gate. I turned around and there she was, ever so gorgeous, standing and looking at me. I couldn't move, and neither could I take my eyes off her. An iota of a smile followed which quietly vanished and turned into a tear. She refused to let it flow down as she looked the other way and steadied herself. Without a word spoken, she walked towards me, and then past me. She unlocked the door, and I stood behind her, a few inches away. The distance between us was so little, and yet, I felt I was miles away.

She went inside her house, and I stood there confused. I was hesitant to go inside without her permission, and neither did I want to go away. I stood there, waiting further, to get an indication from her, but then there was none. I felt the hatred in her. I had no option but to leave, without wanting to. I turned back and took a few steps towards the gate. As I reached the gate, out of one last hope, I looked back at the door, and I found her standing there. This time, I forced a smile onto my face, and it got a similar response from her. Perhaps, this lightened my guilt, and I took the courage to go towards her.

In a moment of craze accompanied with a touch of guilt, I kneeled down in front of her and said, "Sorry."

She burst into laughter and said, "Rahul, you wouldn't change, would you?"

Her laughter was a great moment of relief for me and eased me into a conversation.

"Come inside," she said, and she walked into her living room. I followed her.

Sorrow seemed to have become synonymous with the house in the years that passed by. A shade of darkness filled the house. All the windows and curtains were closed. This was pretty strange as every single time I had been to her house, I could see the passion for house maintenance in Sakshi. She was always keen to keep things in order and perfect. She loved to keep the windows open and let the fresh air flow inside her house. This was missing now, and she seemed a completely different person.

"What are you looking at?" Sakshi exclaimed.

"Some things have changed," I replied.

She looked around and said, "Not a single wall frame or flower vase has changed."

I smiled and replied, "It is not all about the vases and the frame, isn't it?"

She nodded her head in acceptance.

A pause ensured complete silence. For a moment, it felt like two strangers forced by circumstances surrounding them were speaking to one another. In the past, the words we spoke to one another were not enough. Today, it felt like the opposite. There seemed to be no words to be spoken.

The whole setting between us seemed formal. Every single time our eyes stuck to another, an uneasy smile emanated from her. The smile resonated hurt and not happiness. Lots of questions were stuck onto my brain, but I needed some courage to spell it out.

"So, what are you up to these days?" I asked.

"I mean... job, studies and stuff like that."

"Yeah, I work,' she said, and after a little pause, continued saying, "At Xoox incorporation."

"Okay. Actually cool. Nice company, good job. You have moved on. Good," I replied.

"Time moves on, Rahul, and everyone does along with it."

I knew what she meant, and it was me who brought it on myself.

Chapter Fifteen

"**D**AD passed away, Rahul," she said quietly.

"What!" I exclaimed in disbelief. I was shocked. This was the last thing I wanted to hear.

"Last year. He had a year of struggle before that," she continued speaking without looking at me.

"He struggled all through his life. There was no one around during this time." She shut her eyes for a moment.

"The irony of not marrying someone whom your family doesn't approve, leads to this, isn't it?" she asked softly.

Her eyes had a rim of moisture around, filled by the pain that remained heavy in her heart. She needed someone back then, and I was not there. I wished she had called me all the while, but then why would she?

I wanted to hug her, right there and say that I was always going to be there for her. But she wouldn't trust me. I was feeling uncomfortable.

"This is my world, right now, Rahul." She continued, "Filled with lots of silence."

That very statement expelled the tears of my eyes, and I could no longer hide them from her. She looked at me and felt my discomfort.

Before she could say a word to me, I got up from the place and walked out of her house. The guilt was burning loud inside me, and I had no control over what I was doing. I had no face to show her.

I had barely reached about a hundred meters from her house when I got a WhatsApp message from her.

Sorry.

She texted, and in the next text, she said:

I shouldn't have bothered you with my story.

Was it a prick to my already wounded heart or was it something she felt? Either way, it was tearing me, and I had to reply.

I replied:

It was my mistake

Not once but twice now.

I was now looking at the chat window and was waiting for the blue tick. Within a few seconds, the ticked turned blue. It only meant that she was as well hooked on to the phone waiting for my reply to her message. And now I stood there waiting for her reply. I did not even enter the elevator to my hotel room as I felt there could be a loss in the network.

I was so glued to my mobile that I forgot about the happenings around me.

Sakshi is typing... Followed by a blank and then again... *Sakshi is typing...*

The feeling of a child waiting to see the examination result was flowing within me. Should I preempt a reply from her? Perhaps not, I chose to wait.

And in a few seconds, the reply arrived.

"Which is the second one?"

I was now further puzzled. What did she think to be as the first one?

I took a few seconds, perhaps about a minute or so, before I replied:

> For the one in the past and for today, sorry.

She replied with a smile.

"Holy crap," I yelled to myself. "How could she not even scold me or blame me for all the bad things in her life?" I would have been happier had she done that. Now, I was still repenting for my behaviour.

The very next minute, my cell flashed the arrival of the next message.

> Just forget it. What has happened, has. You had your reasons on that day.

> I did, but that does not justify my behaviour. Sorry for that.

> Never mind.

I was heading nowhere and was standing in the midst of a street with very high traffic. I wanted to talk to her. I was a little nervous to call her. In a few minutes, my phone rang.

"Hello!" said a familiar voice from the other end.

"Hi!"

"Where are you?" she asked in a pleasing and confident tone.

"About a hundred meters from your house, near the Svensers."

"Be right there. In five minutes, I will be there."

❦

"First coffee at a Café Coffee Day in three years," she said.

CCD used to be one of our most favourite hangouts. Every week we would be there and most of our celebrations; be it her winning badminton games or me scoring higher grade, we followed it up with a coffee at CCD.

I smiled and nodded my head in disbelief. It was impossible for me to understand her.

"So how is work?" she asked.

"The same. Nothing's changed at work," I said.

Our conversation began formally yet again, but in no time, it became quite relaxed and informal, like it used to be earlier.

I took a deep breath and waited, and finally asked, "What happened to your dad?"

"Cancer, pancreas," she said. Slowly her voice was breaking, and I could feel that she was going to burst into tears at any moment.

"It was a long struggle by the time he left. I was happy for him. He did not have to struggle any longer. It was diagnosed on the day of his attack. A routine body check found it out." She was conscious of not seeing into my eyes when she was speaking.

There was a long silence between us. And we never looked into each other. I cursed myself further.

"His last moment, I was there. A small tear came out if his eyes. He wanted to live for me, like all his life. And when he closed his eyes, I felt the weight of the world around me. I assured him that I would be fine."

And both of us burst into tears.

"And I will be fine," she assured herself yet again.

I could not hold myself back any longer, and I placed my hands on her hand. By then, the coffee arrived, which helped us to lighten the gravity of sorrow around us.

The next few minutes were all about sipping the coffee. The moment needed some silence to comfort ourselves. And then we were off.

We walked outside the cafe and now needed some direction to take the next step together. I wanted to explain to her, as to why I behaved the way I did, the last time. But then, I was too silly to justify my stand.

"How about a short walk?" I asked her.

"Just a short one," she quizzed.

"Depends on you." I smiled and replied back.

"Maybe next time, Rahul."

"Just a few minutes, Sakshi. A really short one. I promise," I pleaded.

And she nodded her head in acceptance.

The sun was burning our skin and the precipitation was setting in. The clouds were beginning to set in, and the rains were about two hours away. Walking was no fun in the crowded traffic, and with disconnected footpaths all over the place, we decided to take one of the residential streets in the inners of Indiranagar.

"So, why are you here in Bangalore?"

I wished she had not asked me that question. I had no answer to tell. If I say that I came for her, she would not believe.

After a prolonged pause, I replied, "Long hours in the office, and after three years, my body and soul needed a break."

She looked at me with attention. For a moment, it felt like she was judging whether I was telling the truth or a lie.

"And so, why Bangalore?" she quizzed further.

"Well, maybe for some soul searching," I replied, and a pause ensued between us.

After a long silence, and a few meters of walking, she spoke, but this time, her voice was shrill.

"I wanted to ask you this whenever I met you again in my life," she said.

I looked at her and nodded my head. The pace of our walking had slowed down a little bit.

"What was my mistake? Why do people find it easy to leave me and move away?" she continued.

I looked at her in disdain. I knew I had no answers, but she wouldn't let me get away without answering her.

She could sense my discomfort with the question and tried to ease her tone a little bit.

"I am not trying to blame you. Please, don't get me wrong. But I need some answers about this," she said as we now stopped walking and stood still facing one another.

I looked away, but not for too long. And finally, I replied, "I had explained my situation to you the other day."

She immediately interrupted me as soon as I started to explain my position.

"Rahul, Rahul. Stop," she said.

"It is not about you, Rahul. It is about me. I want to know why people leave me. And not about why you left me."

I cleared my throat and said, "You are too sweet, Sakshi. Too much love and care is hard to digest, and that is what people get from you. People probably leave you because they wouldn't want to hurt you being with you."

"Meaning?" she asked.

"It was only a few days later, after that incident when I realized that what happened, happened for good."

She had a puzzled look on her face, but for sure, she was listening every bit of it.

"Had I been around you all these years, I would have possibly hurt you a lot."

She smiled at me. It was more of a jibe, and she said, "You think you didn't by not being with me?"

The grief in her tone was apparent, and the power of that one statement was immense, to an extent that she was almost about to explode into tears.

Her phone started to ring, which indeed, helped in breaking the uneasy conversation. She cut the call the first time, but as we started to walk, her phone rang once again.

She picked up the call, and said, "Yes, Aryan. I will be there in a few minutes."

On that note, she turned to me and said, "I have to leave, Rahul. It is time and it was very nice of you to come and meet me. I will call you. Take care."

And she left without waiting for my acknowledgement.

Chapter Sixteen

I WAS caught in the midst of nowhere. And she left me, with me having to wait for a call from her. Right now, my mind was shifting focus towards Aryan.

Aryan, as much as I knew of him, was stalking her during the college days. He was not someone who troubled her. He genuinely liked her and even proposed to her once. However, Sakshi gently rejected his proposal back then. Thoughts of what could have changed in the days I was not around were hurting me.

What if she moved on in her life and found someone else. Did she even need me? Should I just move away from her and give her some space? I don't deserve her for sure. I was the one who was selfish in leaving her.

Two hours passed by, and I did not receive a call from her. I kept staring at my phone for as long as I could. I kept the ringtone volume to the maximum and was hoping that I would get a call from her soon. I kept checking the signal strength to ensure that there were no signal issues. The anxiety in me was growing, and by now, the thoughts within me were killing me. I did not want to call her as that would be too impolite. She promised she would call back, and I had to wait for her call.

Two hours led to four, and still there wasn't a word from her. I was not sure whether she had moved on in her life, but by now, it was clear to me that the wait was meaningless. I wanted to get back to Chennai as soon as I could. I was no longer able to bear the pain, and in haste, I packed my bag and started to walk towards the reception of the hotel. As soon as I picked my mobile, I heard the tone I was waiting for.

"Dinner at Story Wall?"

ॐ

It was 7 p.m, and I was waiting at the entrance of the Metro station at M.G Road. The idea was to pick her up from there and then walk to the Story Wall Café, which was a few hundred meters away. I was waiting for her and was making sure that I did not miss her in the crowd. It took a few minutes to find her. I could only see a few glimpses of her initially. She was wearing a yellow salwar which was lighting her fair skin beautifully. Even the little glimpse of her felt like she had wrapped her arms around the soul of my world. There was no one I loved more, and I did not ever want to miss her. I loved her softness, and she was the most astonishing girl I had ever met. It was her eyes that showed her soul, and they were beaming with joy. I could see her smiling happily and talking to someone else as she was walking towards me. I strolled a few steps ahead to see my fears coming true.

Aryan and Sakshi were walking together towards me, and all I did was to turn away. I had the feeling of being thrown away from a high cliff. The excitement within me turned into sorrow, and it was harder for me to control the tears from flowing out of my eyes. I wanted to cry out loud. My heart was bursting in pain, and I had no means to let them out. Just then, like every fairy moment before, the rains arrived.

I stepped out to cover my tears beneath the raindrops and let out a couple of deep breaths to stabilize myself. The last one minute was like a roller coaster ride leading me into a fire. Before I was immersed completely into the ashes, I heard her calling me out in the distance. She stayed back at a distance to keep herself dry from the rains. By now, the rains were pouring harder, and how I wished I could have chosen to get drenched on the day I first met her. I steadied myself and turned around to look at her, and never once before, I have seen her as happy as she was. Despite the sorrow within me, I could not resist admiring her understated beauty, and this was further pushing out tears. But for the rains, I would have stood embarrassed. I could see the love in her eyes, and I dared not to look at them one more time. I only wished it was because of me. As the rains continued to batter me, I froze.

"Rahul?" Sakshi said.

"Hi, Sakshi."

"Is everything okay?"

"Yes, why do you ask?" I said with pain and anxiety in my voice.

"You are getting yourself drenched in rain."

"Nothing. I love it," I replied, trying to hide my sorrow from her.

"Glad that you are here, Rahul," she said.

"I have something important to tell you today, and that is why I asked you to come," she continued.

I nodded my head and, by now, I was pretty sure what she was going to say. I did not want to hear the obvious from her. I couldn't take it any longer, and I wanted to leave that place immediately. My mind was searching for some reasons to get away from the place immediately but found none.

"This is Aryan," she said, turning towards him.

I shook his hands and acknowledged him.

"For the last two years, if there was one person who stood by me, it was him. If not for him, I was well lost."

I could only smile with my soul disappearing in front of me. To my rescue, my phone rang. I excused myself and walked a few steps away to pick the call.

Maahi was my savior. She wanted to check on me. I informed her that I would call her back. Although it was a short call, it was a good enough opportunity for me to use it as an excuse to get away.

"Sakshi, I am sorry," I said, and continued, "I have to leave now. There is something I need to work on urgently."

I turned to Aryan and said, "Sorry. Glad to meet you," and exchanged a quick smile with him and left the place without hearing a word from either of them.

I came down a few steps of the metro station, and thankfully an auto-rickshaw was waiting for me. I got into it, and for one last time, I turned around to look at her.

She was gorgeous, standing there with him and how beautiful she looked.

They both look good as a pair, I said to myself.

He was probably the right fit for her. I promised myself that I would never ever trouble her again in my life. The only solace I had was to see her happy, and she was with him.

A tear flowed down my cheeks as the auto moved ahead.

Chapter Seventeen

BANGALORE rains and it had been pouring for the last few hours. The roads looked more like a river. It was hard to find out whether you were stepping on a drain or on a road. It was not possible to leave to Chennai as all the trains were stopped or running late due to the rains. The roads were not a good option either.

For a second, while sitting on the couch in the hotel, I thought of calling Sakshi, but somehow resisted. Soon, I got a call from Sakshi. I couldn't stop myself from picking the call.

"Where are you?" she asked.

"At the hotel. About to leave, Sakshi."

"Will you come for me, one last time, to M.G Road Boulevard? I am waiting here for you."

In all these years, my expectation from Sakshi was to not behave coldly at time. She would hardly be bothered about it.

"This is my last chance to win back your trust, isn't it?" I asked.

We didn't fight like couples, but there were tensions that needed to be talked about. I have never ever complained about her behaviour, and neither did she.

"Perhaps." And she hung up the call.

What I appreciated from her the most was that she didn't pretend to be bossy, and she never tried to change my mind. Today, her tone felt different.

The rains continued to pour in, and I needed to find a way to get to Boulevard, which was about 4 kms away. It was hard to get a taxi or an auto. With the roads filled with water, no one wanted to take a risk. Bangalore had never looked so miserable to me. The clouds were behaving like an angry brat who'd do anything to spoil your life. Hell had descended on Bangalore today, and I chose to walk the distance.

I preferred walking on the sidepaths to avoid manholes. Part of the city was in darkness, and I was wondering what Sakshi was doing at Boulevard right now. I was getting worried about her.

As I walked in the water, my heartbeats were getting faster.

"What if I failed to reach her?"

My worst fear was being real. Walking in almost three feet of water, with lots of dirt and drains all around was obstructing my destiny. I shut my brains and eyes towards them as I continued to march faster. Now and then, I saw a lot of cars stuck on the roads with water in their engine. Roads were getting closed, and people were yelling at each other to stay clear from water.

It was dark, and there was water all around, and I couldn't believe what I was doing amidst all this.

"She is waiting for me," I kept saying to myself.

By now, my mobile phone had water seeping into it and got switched off. I couldn't contact her. I was tired of walking, but couldn't stop. As soon as I reached Boulevard, I could see her standing under a shed, which couldn't keep her all dry.

As soon as she saw me, she ran a couple of steps towards me and then slowed down. She looked worried and tensed.

"So, you have braved the rains and come for me," she said.

'It was my last chance, isn't it?' I asked as I saw the expression change on her face.

"Why is it that you always love keeping me worried?" she asked.

I knew what she was referring to, and I took the phone from my dripping pocket and gave it to her.

"This had to happen. Right?" she said.

"Always," I replied.

The sound of thunder was deafening to our ears, and the rain with all its might was shoeing us away. We feared not.

"Why did you run away today, Rahul?" she asked as she looked straight into my eyes. The way she looked into my eyes suggested to me that she needed the truth.

I looked away, as I said, "I had to go. Something urgent had cropped up."

She held my hand and insisted, "I can read your eyes, and you know it. Tell me the truth."

How could I say to you that I can't see you with any other person? I said to myself.

She kept insisting me over and over, and I finally said, "It was because of Aryan, Sakshi. I had thought only two of us were meeting."

She knew that this was coming. She wanted to hear it out from me. Expecting someone to say something is different from actually hearing it from them. She always preferred to hear it and then from thereon.

She turned away and looked towards Cubbon Park.

"You hated me when I said I was lost without him. Isn't it?"

I couldn't deny it, and she was right.

"You have this habit of assuming and making decisions yourself, which is why I hate you, Rahul," she said in agony.

"I heard some things all along, Sakshi, and I didn't believe it until I saw you both together. And I am here now because I still do not believe in it," I said honestly.

She paused for a while and said, "There is no doubt that he loves me. He had proposed to me in college, and you were there. When my dad had passed away, I had no one to speak to. He used to talk to me once in a while."

I listened to her patiently as the rains healed a little, but the winds picked up. The cool winds were making us shiver more.

"You don't know how it feels to be all alone, Rahul. He used to remind me that I was alive. I know that I wasn't all fair to you. I asked you to go away, and I'm sorry for that. It was the moment. I always wanted you to be with me," she said.

Was she saying that she was in a relationship with him? I kept thinking. But I knew I had to wait till she completed speaking her heart out. I was getting prepared for it mentally.

"I understand, Sakshi. And I was foolish enough to keep myself away all the while. I didn't want to trouble you. How did I even believe that you hated me?" I said.

"He helped me find a job and earn for myself. But beyond this, he did something that I will remember all my life," she said, and I didn't say anything.

"When I was feeling low and missed my dearest friend, it was him who came to me and assured me that you would come someday. It was that day that he won a lot of respect from me. I asked him to come over today to show him that you have come." She didn't have to justify herself, but she did because I was hurt.

Was it a sense of relief in me or was it a feeling of pain, I didn't know in that moment, but I felt different. I was bleeding with a lot of emotions inside my heart, and I loved her all the more.

"I am sorry, and I need to pierce myself for getting used to saying sorry to you, Sakshi," I said.

She smiled and said, "You have walked four kilometres in this rain. You had come all the way for me from Chennai. And we are standing here, shivering and wet, in this rain. Is it because I want to hear a sorry from you, Rahul?"

This one statement shook me off completely. I wanted to say it out today, and loudly. Before I could, she looked at me and said, "I can see it in your eyes. Every moment, right from day one. Even now, I can see it. I don't know if you remember what my dad said the first time you met him. Even he knew it." The words were falling out from her heart, one after another.

"But you have always failed me. Today, I feel you know nothing of me. Every time we were together, I used to feel you would tell me, and I kept waiting. Even today, when you came, I thought you will say it. But, instead, you chose to leave." And she started crying. She poured out all that she had kept inside her for years.

I walked closer to her and said, "In all these years, I was worried about only one thing. The thought of you leaving me.

But today, I know that no matter what happens, we are meant to be together all our lives."

The way we looked into each other's eyes was the happiness we both were waiting for. The day had finally come, and we both and found each other forever. The rains were set aside by the overflowing love for each other. In the heavy rains, we were like the little stars entering in their own galaxies.

I looked at her, and she looked at me. And finally, I hugged her and lifted her. She looked from above me and said, "You wouldn't say it, even now, right?"

And I nodded my head, and we both smiled.